Single D!

At work
profession
walk in the door, these single dads take
on full-time fatherhood duty!

**These devoted dads still find room
in their lives for love…**

It takes very special women to win the hearts
of these dedicated doctors, and a very special
kind of caring to make these single fathers
full-time husbands!

Jennifer Taylor lives in the north-west of England with her husband Bill. She had been writing Mills & Boon® romances for some years, but when she discovered Medical Romances™ she was so captivated by these heart-warming stories that she set out to write them herself! When not writing, or doing research for her latest book, Jennifer's hobbies include reading, travel, walking her dog and retail therapy (shopping!). Jennifer claims all that bending and stretching to reach the shelves is the best exercise possible. She's always delighted to hear from readers, so do visit her at www.jennifer-taylor.com

Recent titles by the same author:

THE CONSULTANT'S ADOPTED SON
   Bachelor Dads
IN HIS LOVING CARE *Bachelor Dads*
NURSE IN A MILLION*
THE FOREVER ASSIGNMENT*
A SPECIAL KIND OF CARING

*Worlds Together

A BABY OF HIS OWN

BY
JENNIFER TAYLOR

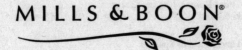

MILLS & BOON®

DID YOU PURCHASE THIS BOOK WITHOUT A COVER?

If you did, you should be aware it is **stolen property** as it was reported *unsold and destroyed* by a retailer. Neither the author nor the publisher has received any payment for this book.

All the characters in this book have no existence outside the imagination of the author, and have no relation whatsoever to anyone bearing the same name or names. They are not even distantly inspired by any individual known or unknown to the author, and all the incidents are pure invention.

All Rights Reserved including the right of reproduction in whole or in part in any form. This edition is published by arrangement with Harlequin Enterprises II B.V. The text of this publication or any part thereof may not be reproduced or transmitted in any form or by any means, electronic or mechanical, including photocopying, recording, storage in an information retrieval system, or otherwise, without the written permission of the publisher.

This book is sold subject to the condition that it shall not, by way of trade or otherwise, be lent, resold, hired out or otherwise circulated without the prior consent of the publisher in any form of binding or cover other than that in which it is published and without a similar condition including this condition being imposed on the subsequent purchaser.

MILLS & BOON and MILLS & BOON with the Rose Device are registered trademarks of the publisher.

First published in Great Britain 2006
Harlequin Mills & Boon Limited,
Eton House, 18-24 Paradise Road, Richmond, Surrey TW9 1SR

© Jennifer Taylor 2006

ISBN 0 263 84741 1

Set in Times Roman 10½ on 12¾ pt
03-0706-53860

Printed and bound in Spain
by Litografia Rosés, S.A., Barcelona

CHAPTER ONE

'YOU'RE never going to believe what's happened!'

Staff Nurse Lucy Adams glanced round as the staffroom door burst open. It was Lucy's first day back at work on Dalverston General's paediatric unit following her maternity leave. She had been hoping to ease herself back into the job after several months' absence, but it had been far too busy as one crisis had succeeded another. She'd not had time to stop for any lunch and had been making herself a cup of coffee when her friend, Sandra Clark, had appeared. Now she groaned as she saw the excitement on the other nurse's face.

'I'm not sure if I want to hear this.'

'Oh, yes, you do!' Sandra grimaced when she heard foot-steps coming along the corridor. It was obvious that she wanted to tell Lucy her news before they were interrupted. 'Guess who they've hired to replace Mark Dawson?'

'I've no idea and I really don't care so long as he or she can do the job,' Lucy assured her, sinking down onto a chair. 'It's been bedlam in here this morning. I don't know how they expect us to cope with half our staff missing—'

'Connor Mackenzie!'

Lucy froze so that the cup of coffee that had been on its

way to her mouth ended up suspended in mid-air. Sandra laughed in delight.

'I *knew* you'd be surprised! I was stunned when I found out, too. I never thought Connor would come back here to work, did you?'

'No. I didn't.' It was hard to force the words past the knot of panic in her throat but Lucy knew that she mustn't let Sandra see how shocked she really was. Nobody knew about her and Connor—they'd gone to great lengths to keep their relationship a secret. Gossip was rife in any hospital and they hadn't wanted everyone talking about them.

In the event, Lucy had been glad they'd been so careful. At least she'd been spared the embarrassment of people knowing that Connor had cared more about his career than he'd cared about her. And because nobody knew they'd had an affair, they hadn't put two and two together when she'd announced that she was pregnant. Isabel was six months old now and nobody—not even Lucy's own family—knew that Connor was her father. That was how she intended it to remain, too. So far as she was concerned, Connor Mackenzie had no claim on her precious daughter.

'At least we're getting someone with experience to take over the post.' She fixed a smile to her mouth, hoping it would convince Sandra that the news didn't worry her. Of course it did, because working with Connor was going to be very awkward, but she had to start as she meant to go on. 'It was a real blow when Mark decided to accept that position in Cambridge, but Connor's an excellent doctor. And he's great with the kids, too.'

'He's also gorgeous and sexy in case you've forgotten.' Sandra gave a little chuckle. 'Or have your hormones not recovered yet from the joys of childbirth?'

'My hormones are fine, thank you very much,' Lucy retorted, knowing that she had to play along—it was expected of her.

Her heart suddenly skipped a beat as a picture of Connor appeared in her mind's eye: that crisp black hair, those wonderful green eyes and chiselled features. He *was* gorgeous, and sexy, and a host of other things as well, but none of those mattered. It was Izzy who was the most important person in her life now, and Izzy's happiness was her only concern. She wasn't going to allow her daughter's feelings to be trampled on by a man who put his career before everything else!

The thought steadied her so that she was able to smile more naturally this time. 'I'm just too tired from looking after a teething baby all night to appreciate Connor Mackenzie's finer points.'

'Then you must be the only woman in this hospital who feels that way.' Sandra gave a little shudder. 'Oh, this must be my lucky day. I was *gutted* when Connor left to work in the States. I never thought he'd come back to Dalverston once he'd had a taste of the good life. It must be fate is all I can say. Pure fate!'

Lucy laughed sceptically. 'Or bad luck, you mean. Connor might be good-looking but he's too wrapped up in his precious career to care about anything else. You could find yourself at the end of a long line of disappointed females who wish they'd never heard of the wonderful Dr Mackenzie!'

She looked up, expecting Sandra to refute that claim, and suddenly realised there was someone standing in the doorway. Her breath caught as she realised who it was. He gave her a thin smile as he came into the room but she could see the anger in his green eyes and a shiver raced through her. She wasn't sure if it had been that disparaging comment that had upset him, but there was no doubt at all that Connor Mackenzie was furiously angry.

'Obviously, you're not my number one fan, Staff Nurse Adams. Whilst you're perfectly entitled to your views, I do hope you'll keep any remarks like that to yourself in future. I would prefer it if my staff at least pretended to show me some respect.'

Colour washed up Lucy's face as she quickly stood up. Maybe Connor was within his rights to chastise her, but there was no way she was going to allow him to walk all over her. 'I apologise, Dr Mackenzie. Obviously, that remark wasn't intended for your ears. I shall be more careful in future.'

'Thank you.' His eyes bored into her as he narrowed the gap between them. 'Harmony within my team is something I value very highly. If you have a grievance, I expect you to tell me about it. Is that clear?'

'Perfectly,' she retorted, her brown eyes blazing back at him. Maybe she couldn't put her feelings into words but there was no way he wouldn't understand the message she was trying to convey. He might be her boss now, not her lover, but she resented him pulling rank this way.

'Good.' An ironic smile curled his mouth. 'It's best to get things out into the open, I find. It saves a lot of confusion. Trying to keep secrets rarely works.'

Lucy wasn't sure what he meant by that. To anyone listening, it would appear that he was laying down some ground rules before he took up the post as head of the paediatric unit. However, she sensed there'd been a deeper meaning behind the words and it worried her. Was Connor warning her that he'd found out about Izzy?

Panic swept over her at the thought of him knowing about

her daughter and she turned away, terrified that he would see just how scared she was. She emptied the rest of her coffee down the sink and hurried to the door. Sandra was chatting to Connor now so with a bit of luck she should be able to slip away. She just needed a few minutes to calm herself down and then she'd be able to deal with whatever Connor threw at her.

'Could I have a word with you before you go back to the ward, Lucy?'

She was almost out of the door when Connor called her back and for a moment she was tempted to ignore him. However, she knew it would create more problems if she did that. No matter how she felt about him personally, he was still her boss.

'We're short-staffed today,' she told him crisply.

'So I believe. I was informed at my interview that staffing levels are at an all-time low. It's something I intend to rectify as soon as possible.'

He turned to Sandra and Lucy's mouth pursed with distaste when she saw the dazzling smile he bestowed on the other woman. 'I know you're supposed to go off duty soon, but I really need to have a word with Lucy. Would you mind covering for her just this once?'

'Of course I don't mind, Connor—I mean, Dr Mackenzie,' Sandra amended hastily.

'Thanks. And Connor will do fine.' He gave her another megawatt smile. 'I can't see the point of standing on ceremony when we're all here for the same reason. Make sure everyone knows that, will you?'

'Of course!'

Sandra glided out of the room, an expression of such bliss on her face that it made Lucy's stomach churn. Something of what she was feeling must have shown on her face because Connor laughed.

'A bit of charm works wonders, I find. It's far more effective than rattling out orders.'

'I'm sure you're right.' Lucy came back into the room although she didn't sit down when he waved her towards a chair. 'I prefer to stand, thank you. You did say this wouldn't take long.'

'It won't.' He closed the door and turned to face her. 'What I have to say can be said in very few words, although I'm sure you would prefer it to be said in private.'

'I can't imagine what you and I have to talk about of a private nature,' she countered. 'Our relationship ended when you went to America. You made it very clear it was the end, too. What was it you said on our last evening together? Ah, yes, I remember now. There was no point keeping in touch because you preferred to make a clean break. You then told me to get on with my life and that you hoped I'd be happy. Well, I'm glad to say that I took your advice on both counts.'

'So I believe.' He leant against the door and there was something about the way he was looking at her that made a shiver run down her spine. 'I bumped into Lisa Saunders a few weeks ago. She was in Boston for a seminar so we spent a couple of hours catching up. It was a surprise to hear that she and Will were married, although that wasn't her only news, of course. She also told me that you were on maternity leave. Your baby is how old now…six months?'

Lucy nodded. She was too afraid to speak. She had the most awful feeling that she knew where this was leading and was terrified that she would say something to confirm his suspicions. That was all they were, of course—suspicions. Nobody apart from her knew the truth.

'Did I ever tell you that maths was one of my favourite subjects at school? I used to enjoy working out all those problems the teachers set us.' Connor's tone was light and breezy, as though they were indulging in a pleasant little chat. However, the expression in his eyes told a very different story.

'How fascinating,' she replied curtly, desperate not to hear anything else. Even though she had no idea what his liking for maths had to do with the situation, it was unlikely that he was making small-talk for the fun of it. 'Unfortunately, I don't have time to listen to you reminiscing about your schooldays. I need to get back to work.'

'Of course you do. As a single mother, your job must be very important to you. Babies are expensive, aren't they? They need all sorts of things—nappies, clothes, toys—the list must be endless.' He sighed. 'It must be hard enough when the child's father is around to share the burden but when you're on your own—like you, Lucy—it must be a real problem.'

'I manage,' she snapped.

'I'm sure you do. But why should you have to manage by yourself when the baby's father should be doing his bit to help you?' He stepped away from the door and there was something intimidating about the way he was looking at her now. 'He does know about the baby, doesn't he? I know you read about women who go off and have a baby without telling the father, but you wouldn't do a thing like that, would you, Lucy?'

'Isabel's father has nothing whatsoever to do with you!' she shot back, desperate to convince him that she was telling the truth.

'Isabel. So that's what you called her? Lisa couldn't remember her name when I asked her what it was. She just knew you'd had a little girl.' His voice had softened, the harshness replaced by a tenderness that made Lucy's heart suddenly ache. Either he was a superb actor or he really was moved by the thought of her daughter.

Just for a moment, she allowed herself the luxury of imagining how he would react if she told him the truth about Izzy being his child. She could actually picture the smile that would light his handsome face and the way his eyes would fill with love for their daughter—as once upon a time she'd imagined they had filled with love for her.

The thought was like a dash of cold water, returning her with sickening speed to the reality of the situation. And the reality was that Connor allowed nothing to come before his precious career. Nothing had ever mattered as much and nothing ever would, neither a woman nor a child. The thought helped her harden her heart.

'Is this leading somewhere?' She gave him a mocking smile. 'So far we've covered your schooldays, your meeting with Lisa, and the fact that I have a baby. So what else do you wish to discuss?'

'Nothing very much. I've covered the main topics.' He gave a throaty laugh. 'Funnily enough, they're all linked. Meeting Lisa was the start, you see, then came the maths. It was easy enough to subtract the months until I got back to the beginning, which was when your baby was conceived. Correct me if I'm wrong but I'd guess it was April last year. If Isabel is six months old, it would have to be around that time unless she was premature, and Lisa didn't mention that.'

'I'm not listening to this,' Lucy began, but he carried on as though she'd never spoken.

'So assuming that Isabel went to term that means April is right. A lot of things happened that April, as I recall. We spent a lot of time together, including that weekend in Scotland. In fact, if you factor in work—which brings me back to the maths again—then I'd say you had very little opportunity to see anyone else when you were spending so much time with me. *Ipso facto,* Isabel must be my daughter. Am I right, Lucy? Or have my powers of deduction failed me this time?'

Lucy didn't know what to say. She couldn't even claim that it was like having her worst nightmare come true because she'd never dreamt that she and Connor would have this conversation. Since the night they'd parted she'd not heard a word from him—not even a card at Christmas. He had walked out of her life and that had been it. Now she had no idea how to deal with what was happening and her confusion must have shown.

'I don't know what you're planning on doing but, please, don't bother trying to lie your way out of this. It would be a mistake, because I'm not in the mood to listen to any lies. We both know that Isabel is my daughter. She couldn't possibly be anyone else's.'

'Why not? I could have been seeing someone else while we were going out together.' She stared back at him, desperately trying to hold onto her control. She had no idea why he was even interested that he had a child but something warned her that no good would come of it.

'Not you, Lucy. It's not something you'd do.'

The certainty in his voice almost tipped her over the edge and she had to breathe deeply to control her panic.

'Isn't it?' She gave a mocking laugh and was pleased to see his eyelids flicker. Was he having doubts about her faithfulness, wondering if she might have been two-timing him? She hoped so, she really did. Connor Mackenzie needed taking down a peg or two!

'Are you sure about that, Connor? You might be able to account for a large proportion of my time that April but you weren't with me every single minute, were you? There were a number of nights when you were working and I was off duty. Do you know with absolute certainty what I was doing on those nights?'

'No, I don't. I wasn't keeping tabs on you.'

'Exactly!' She laughed again, playing the role of her life. It was vital she convinced him that he couldn't be Isabel's father. Nothing was going to hurt her precious little girl and if that meant denying Connor's paternity, that was what she would do.

'You haven't the faintest idea what went on when you were at work. You didn't really care. Your job has always come first and I don't imagine it would have worried you if you'd found out I was seeing someone else.'

'So who was he, then?' His voice grated but apart from that he seemed unmoved by the fact that she'd claimed to have been having an affair while they'd been seeing each other.

Lucy felt a knot of pain twist her heart but she couldn't afford to admit that it hurt to know how little she'd meant to him. 'Just someone I met one night in a club.'

'So it was a one-night stand—is that what you're saying?'

'That's right. I haven't seen him since and I don't expect to. He was in Dalverston on business and there's no reason to imagine I'll run into him again.'

'And does he have a name? Or didn't you bother asking him that?'

He smiled at her, his white teeth gleaming, his eyes sparkling with what looked like amusement. Was he relieved to have been let off the hook? she wondered, feeling sickly. Glad that another man was the father of her child so that he wouldn't have to worry about the responsibilities of being a parent? The thought was almost too much to bear, but she had to bear it for Izzy's sake.

'I don't see what difference it makes what his name is. He's not part of the equation, to use your own analogy.'

'And you're perfectly happy about that, are you? You don't care that your daughter is going to grow up without knowing her father?'

'A lot of children don't have any contact with one or other of their parents these days. I'm quite sure that it won't make a lot of difference to Isabel's life.'

It wasn't true, of course. She *did* worry about what her daughter was going to miss as she grew up. Her own childhood had been idyllic and she hated to think that Izzy wouldn't enjoy the support that came from a secure family background. However, there was no way that she was prepared to admit that to Connor, especially when he'd accepted her story about another man so readily. If she'd fostered any hopes that he'd ever loved her, they'd just been completely dashed.

The thought was so painful that Lucy knew she had to bring the conversation to an end. She looked pointedly at her watch. 'I need to get back. We're two members of staff down today so we're working at full stretch.'

'Of course. I'm sorry to have delayed you but I'm glad we've had this chat. It's helped to clear up a few things which have been bothering me since I spoke to Lisa.'

He stepped away from the door, but instead of moving out of her way so she could leave, he stopped directly in front of her. Lucy felt her heart start to race when she saw how grim he looked. There was no sign of amusement on his face now and no hint of softness in his voice either.

'The thing I always admired about you, Lucy, was your honesty. You said what you meant and you meant what you said, but obviously you've changed.'

'I don't know what you mean,' she began, but he shook his head.

'Of course you do. You would never have told me that pack of lies about Isabel's father a year ago. There was no other man and we both know that. *I'm* her father and I don't know if I can ever forgive you for trying to hide her existence from me, but I do know that things are going to change from now on.

'She's my daughter as well as yours and I intend to play a proper role in her life. So if you're harbouring any thoughts of cutting me out then I suggest you forget them. I shall do whatever it takes to be a real father to that little girl. And if that means taking you to court to gain access to her, that's what I'll do.'

'Connor…!' she began, but he'd already turned away. Lucy pressed her hand to her mouth as he strode out of the door. She'd always believed that she'd been right not to tell him about Izzy but it didn't feel that way any more. It felt as though she'd not only let her daughter down but Connor as well, which was crazy. She didn't owe him any allegiance. He'd walked out of her life and he had no right to think that he could come back now and create havoc!

She took a steadying breath. The biggest mistake she could make now would be to panic. Isabel was *her* daughter and she would do whatever it took to protect her. Connor was never going to hurt Izzy the way he had hurt her.

CHAPTER TWO

CONNOR couldn't remember a time when he'd felt so angry. Normally, he had no difficulty controlling his temper. He firmly believed that it was futile to expend energy in such a non-productive fashion, yet he couldn't seem to get a grip as he made his way to the ward. Sandra was coming out of the office and he sighed when he saw her face light up. Although he wasn't vain, he was aware of the impact he had on some of the female members of staff and he really didn't feel like politely fending her off.

'I was just coming to find you!' she exclaimed. 'I know you're not officially on duty yet but—'

'What's happened?' he asked immediately because work had always taken priority over everything else.

Funnily enough, the idea stung and he frowned. He'd never considered his dedication to be a drawback before yet he couldn't help wondering if this situation would have arisen if he'd devoted less time to his career. If he hadn't taken up the post in Boston, for instance, he would have known that Lucy had been pregnant.

The fact that he could even consider the move to Boston as something to regret stunned him, so that it was a moment before he realised that Sandra was looking expectantly at him. Although he hated to admit that he hadn't heard a word she'd said, he didn't have a choice.

'Sorry. I was miles away. It must be the jet-lag. I only arrived last night and I'm still catching up with the time difference. Can you tell me all that again?'

'Of course!'

Sandra smiled forgivingly, making it clear that she would happily repeat the information any number of times he wanted her to. Connor wasn't about to slip up again, however. He listened attentively as she explained that Theatre had just phoned to say they had a problem with a seven-year-old they'd been operating on. Sophie Fisher had been undergoing a routine tonsillectomy when she'd suffered an adverse reaction to the anaesthetic, which had caused her heart to stop. The anaesthetist had managed to restart her heart but she would need careful monitoring for the first twenty-four hours or so.

'Is there a high-dependency bed available?' he asked when Sandra had finished. Opening the paediatric high-dependency unit had been a major coup for his predecessor. High-dependency beds bridged the gap between nursing on a ward and in the intensive care unit—they were invaluable in a case like this where a patient needed extra care.

'They're all free,' Sandra admitted. 'We had to close the unit at the beginning of May because we didn't have enough staff to cover it.'

'Are you saying that there's been no high-dependency paediatric beds available for over two months?' he exclaimed incredulously.

'Yes. Oh, they've advertised the posts several times, but

I'm not sure if they've found anyone suitable yet. Maybe Lucy will know. Here she is now, you can ask her.'

Connor glanced round and saw Lucy coming along the corridor. He beckoned her over, pretending not to notice the strain on her face. Even though he was furious about the way she'd cut him out of his daughter's life, it upset him to see her looking so worried.

'We've a seven-year-old girl who needs a high-dependency bed,' he explained crisply, determined not to let his feelings show. 'Sandra has just informed me that the unit is closed.'

'That's right. The staff who were working there have been moved to ICU. Apparently, there were vacancies there as well so the management decided to close the unit and save on resources.'

'That's something I need to sort out,' he said grimly. 'However, it doesn't solve our current problem. How long will it take to prepare a bed in the unit?'

'Not very long. Everything is still in place so it's just a matter of making up a bed and plugging in the equipment. However, there's just three of us on today and Sandra will be going off duty soon. I'm the only one who's done the extra training needed to work in the high-dependency unit and I can't leave the ward.'

'I understand that, but what if I find another nurse to cover the unit? Could you manage then?'

'Yes, of course, although I don't know where you're going to find anyone. There's nobody available in ICU—I've already asked them.'

She shrugged, her brown eyes meeting his for a second before they skittered away. Connor suddenly wished with all his heart that things had turned out differently. If he'd stayed

in Dalverston, he and Lucy would never have been at loggerheads like this, he thought sadly.

Once again the fact that he regretted what had been an excellent career move startled him. His career had always been
the most important thing in his life and to experience these
doubts was deeply unsettling. He turned away, not wanting
her to see how vulnerable he felt all of a sudden.

'Sandra, can you get back on to Theatre and tell them to
send the patient up as soon as they're happy to move her?' He
went to the desk and picked up the phone, glancing at Lucy
over his shoulder. 'And can you get everything ready? The
child's stable at the moment but there's always a chance that
she might suffer a second cardiac arrest and we need to be
prepared for it.'

'But I've just explained that we don't have enough staff to
man the high-dependency unit as well as the ward.'

'And I've just told you that I'll find you another nurse,'
Connor said shortly, keying in the code for an outside line.

'If you can find an experienced critical care nurse in
Dalverston then you must be able to work miracles,' she said
scathingly. 'None of the nursing agencies has anyone suitable
on their books. I know that for a fact because Mark Dawson
told me that he contacted them when he found out the unit was
being closed down.'

'I'm not contacting an agency.' He keyed in another string of
digits, wondering why it hurt to know how little faith she had in
him. He'd never needed anyone's approbation before—he'd
taught himself to be totally self-sufficient—yet he'd have been
lying if he'd claimed that he didn't care how Lucy felt about him.

The thought worried him so much that his tone was
brusquer than it might otherwise have been. 'A friend of mine

from Boston travelled over here with me. She worked in a high-dependency unit so she knows the drill. She qualified in England so there won't be a problem with her nursing credentials either. I'm sure she'll be willing to help if I ask her.'

'I see. I'll leave you to make the arrangements, then.'

Lucy spun round before he could say anything else. Connor frowned as he watched her disappear into the side room that housed the high-dependency beds. She was obviously upset, although he had no idea why. Surely she should be pleased that he'd found a solution to their problem?

His breath caught as a thought struck him. Was it possible that Lucy was jealous? Dee was just a friend and she had her own reasons for coming back to England, but Lucy didn't know that. She probably assumed that Dee was his current girlfriend and that they'd decided to move back here together. He was suddenly overwhelmed by a need to set the record straight, but before he could act on it, Dee answered the phone.

He quickly explained his predicament and, as he'd expected, Dee immediately offered to help. He thanked her and hung up but then he had to clear it with the nursing officer and that caused another delay. By the time everything was arranged, the patient had arrived so once again there was no time to speak to Lucy.

The anaesthetist had brought the girl upstairs himself so they ran through her case notes together. Connor could tell the other man was worried in case any blame might be attached to him, but his notes showed that nothing had happened while Sophie had been in Theatre to have caused her to arrest. It had been a tragic accident caused by an adverse reaction to the anaesthetic agents used during the operation, and he told the anaesthetist that and sent him on his way.

Lucy had the child linked up to the monitoring equipment by the time he went to check on her. She was sedated and connected to a ventilator. Her blood pressure, heart rate and rhythm and oxygen levels were all being monitored. Body fluids and blood-sugar levels were being maintained by intravenous infusions of salts and glucose. Urine was being collected via a catheter and nutrients supplied intravenously. Connor knew that everything possible was being done for the child but as he looked at her pale little face, he was suddenly beset by a pain so intense that he winced.

How would he feel if it was his daughter lying in that bed? It didn't bear thinking about, but it did prove that he'd been right to come back to England. It had been a shock when he'd worked out that Lucy's baby must be his child, too, but he'd known from the outset what he'd had to do.

Isabel was going to grow up knowing that she had a father who loved her. He knew how it felt to be unwanted and wouldn't allow the same thing to happen to his child. He intended to be a proper father to Isabel, not some shadowy figure who drifted in and out of her life, and if Lucy didn't like the idea, it was tough.

He glanced across at Lucy and felt his heart spasm again. He really and truly didn't want to fight with her. Leaving Lucy had been the hardest thing he'd ever had to do, although he doubted if she would believe him if he told her that. It was his own fault because he'd gone to great lengths to ensure that she'd known they hadn't had a future together.

Now the situation had changed, but it wasn't going be easy to persuade her to let him back into her life. It was obvious how she felt about him but he had to find a way to convince her that he didn't mean her or Isabel any harm. He certainly wasn't hoping to rekindle their affair if that was what was worrying her! That was over and done with, although he'd be lying if he claimed that he hadn't thought about her while he'd been in America. There'd been far too many nights, in fact, when he had lain awake, thinking about her. Of all the women he'd ever dated, Lucy was the one who'd touched him most, the one for whom he might have considered abandoning his dreams.

'Sophie Fisher is still giving us cause for concern. Connor has tried her on various drugs but she's not responding as well as he'd hoped she would.'

Lucy handed over the patient's chart to Bea Francis, the night sister, hoping the other woman hadn't noticed the way her voice had quavered when she'd mentioned Connor's name. She took a deep breath to iron out the bumps before continuing.

'She's still showing signs of arrhythmia so he wants the situation monitored overnight. If things haven't settled down by the morning, he'll decide then whether to try cardioversion.'

'It might be the only option,' Bea agreed, glancing at the chart. She set it aside and grinned at Lucy. 'OK, so what's the gen on Connor, then? I was stunned when Mel told me that he was our new boss. Why has he decided to come back to Dalverston?'

'I've no idea.' Lucy shrugged. She didn't want Bea to think she was the least bit bothered by Connor's return. 'Maybe he missed the British weather.'

'You must be joking!'

Bea stared pointedly out of the office window. Despite the fact that it was the middle of July, it was pouring down outside and it had been doing so for a while now. Flood warnings had been posted in the town and the houses closest to the river had been surrounded by a wall of sandbags. It certainly hadn't been the best reason Lucy could have come up with to explain Connor's return but what else could she have said? That he'd come back to claim his daughter?

A spasm ran through her and she rushed on, not wanting to think about how angry he'd been with her. 'I'm sure he must have his reasons for coming back, but who knows what they are?'

'Think they have anything to do with that nurse he's brought in to help?' Bea looked expectantly at her. 'Mel told me they used to work together in Boston. Maybe *she* wanted to come back to England and Connor decided he couldn't bear to lose her so came back as well.'

'It's one theory,' Lucy conceded, although she doubted it was true. Oh, she didn't dispute that Connor and Dee might be having a relationship—how could she when everything pointed towards it? However, it seemed far more likely that Dee had been the one to follow Connor back to England. She couldn't imagine him going anywhere at someone else's behest. Whatever Connor wanted always came first, and other people were expected to fall in with his wishes.

The thought was more than a little scary in the circumstances so she decided it was time to cut short the conversation. 'That's just about everything now so I'll be off. Have a good night.'

'I'll try.' Bea smiled sympathetically as Lucy hurried to the door. 'I expect you're anxious to see Isabel. I remember how much I hated leaving my kids when they were little, but needs must. And at least you were able to get her into the hospital's crèche. That must have made life a bit easier.'

'It was a godsend, them opening it just before I was due to return to work,' Lucy agreed. 'I don't know how I'd have managed if I'd had to take Izzy to a childminder before I came into work this morning. It's amazing how much stuff one small baby needs!'

'It doesn't get any better when they're teenagers,' Bea retorted. 'The essentials just get bigger and more expensive!'

'Thanks! That's really cheered me up.'

Lucy was still laughing when she left the office. She hurried along the corridor, bypassing the nursing station and waving when she saw a couple of members of the night staff behind the desk. She knew that if she stopped to speak to them it would hold her up, and she was anxious to collect Izzy and take her home.

The newly opened staff crèche was in the old part of the building and had taken over the former site of the physiotherapy department. Lucy went straight there but there were still a lot of people ahead of her when she arrived, and she had to queue up to sign in. She'd almost reached the front of the queue when someone tapped her on the shoulder. She turned round and her heart leapt when she found Connor standing behind her.

'What are you doing here?' she demanded, not making any attempt to hide her displeasure.

'What do you think?' He smiled thinly. 'I thought now would be as good a time as any to meet my daughter.'

'Sh! Keep your voice down,' Lucy admonished, frantically looking over his shoulder. Fortunately the woman behind them in the queue was talking to her friend and didn't appear to have heard what he'd said. Nevertheless, she was furious with him for being so indiscreet.

'People are going to find out at some point,' he stated coolly. 'Maybe you would prefer to keep quiet about me being Isabel's father but I have no intention of lying.'

'It isn't up to you, though, Connor. It's my decision what I choose to tell people. And if I prefer not to tell them about you, that's what will happen.'

'Meaning that I don't have a choice in the matter?' He shook his head. 'Sorry, Lucy, but it isn't up to you to make that decision on your own. It's something we need to discuss, along with a lot of other things concerning our daughter.'

'What other things?'

'All sorts of things, and far too many to list at the moment if you don't want anyone overhearing.'

His tone was flat yet she sensed a certain tension about him, which surprised her. It was unlike Connor to display his feelings. He'd always been very cool and contained, keeping his emotions in check—apart from when they'd been sharing their most intimate moments, of course.

The memory of their love-making brought a rush of heat to her cheeks and she turned away, busying herself with signing her name in the visitors' book. Security was tight and only parents or people designated by a parent were allowed inside the crèche. She moved away from the desk, then paused. If Connor tried to follow her, he would have problems getting in. Even though she hated the thought of him meeting Izzy, she didn't want to run the risk of him causing a scene.

'Dr Mackenzie is with me,' she informed the nursery nurse who was standing guard at the door. 'Is it all right if he comes in with me?'

'So long as he signs the book,' the girl agreed. 'Shall I add him to the list of people authorised to see Izzy?'

'No,' Lucy said quickly.

'Yes.' Connor signed his name, ignoring the furious look she shot at him. He treated the girl to one of his most captivating smiles. 'If it isn't too much trouble.'

'Of course not!' The young nursery nurse beamed at him. 'Just fill in this card with your contact details and hand it back to me on your way out. I'll do the rest.'

'Thanks.' Connor pocketed the card then slid his hand under Lucy's elbow and steered her away from the desk. He shook his head when she opened her mouth to protest. 'Save it till later. I don't want Izzy getting upset because she's seen us fighting.'

Lucy's lips clamped together. She couldn't argue with that sentiment, but she resented his high-handed attitude and intended to tell him that as soon as she got the chance.

She shrugged off his hand as they entered the main section of the crèche, which had once housed the physiotherapy department's gymnasium. It had been transformed into an attractive play area now, complete with a large plastic slide and shelves full of toys. A separate room had been set aside for the babies so she went straight there, her face breaking into a smile when she saw Izzy sitting on a rug in the corner. The little girl was happily beating a plastic saucepan with a wooden spoon and Lucy felt a rush of love assail her as she knelt down beside her.

'Hello, darling. Are you having a lovely time?'

Izzy immediately dropped the spoon and held out her arms to be picked up. Lucy lifted her into the air and blew a raspberry on her tummy, feeling her eyes fill with tears as she inhaled the familiar scent of baby powder. Today had been the first time they'd been apart since Izzy had been born and she had missed her so much.

'Aren't you going to introduce us?'

She looked round when Connor spoke and maybe it was because she was already feeling so emotional that a lump came to her throat when she saw the expression on his face. He was staring at Izzy with such wonderment that the coldest heart would have melted.

All of a sudden she felt ashamed of her decision to keep Izzy's existence a secret from him. At the time it had seemed like the right thing to do but it no longer felt that way. And yet if she accepted Connor's role in her daughter's life, she would have to accept him as part of her life, too. Could she cope with being around him on that basis? Or would the strain prove too much?

Her heart began to race but there was no way that she could avoid the truth any longer. She still loved Connor, even though she knew that he had never really loved her.

CHAPTER THREE

'HELLO, IZZY.'

Connor could barely speak for the wealth of emotions that had hit him the moment he'd seen the child. It was strange because he'd never imagined he would experience such an intense reaction. He'd expected to feel something akin to what he felt for the children he treated—he wanted to care for them and make then better—but this was so much more. He couldn't seem to drag his eyes away from her as he crouched down beside her and took stock of every tiny detail.

She had dark hair just like his, he realised in amazement. And huge green eyes, also like his. The rest of her features were exactly like Lucy's, from the delicately arched brows to the sweet little rosebud mouth. He was suddenly struck by the sheer wonder of what they'd done by creating this tiny human being. Izzy had inherited bits of him and bits of Lucy, and the thought that their love-making had resulted in something so perfect shook him to the very core of his being. And yet, was it *really* so surprising?

His gaze moved to Lucy and pain gripped him as the

memories came rushing back. Making love with Lucy had always been a magical experience. He'd had his share of relationships before they'd met, but what he'd felt for her had been far more profound than anything he had experienced before.

It was the reason why he'd taken the job in Boston, in fact. He had always planned on spending another year in Dalverston but he'd realised that he had been getting too involved with her and had been afraid that his career would suffer because of it. Moving to Boston had been the sensible thing to do, yet all of a sudden he found himself wondering if there were more important things than a career—like people to love and who would love him in return. Surely they mattered far more than a job?

Connor took a deep breath. It was only natural that he should feel unsettled, but he mustn't allow it to throw him off course. He tickled Izzy's hand and laughed when she immediately grabbed hold of his fingers. 'She doesn't seem worried about having a stranger touching her.'

'She's not reached the clingy stage yet,' Lucy replied coldly, and he sighed. It was obvious from her tone that she was still angry with him.

'Something to look forward to,' he said lightly. He didn't want her to think that it bothered him to be *persona non grata* in her eyes.

The thought touched an already sensitive nerve and he stood up. He'd spent far too much of his childhood feeling like an outsider to enjoy re-enacting the experience. Lucy started to get up as well and he automatically offered her his hand but she ignored him as she settled the baby onto her hip.

Connor forbore to say anything as he followed her from the room. If there were battles to be fought, he would save his energy until it was needed. However, she didn't know him very well if she thought that he would back down in the face of her continued hostility.

The same nursery nurse was on duty at the door and he groaned when he remembered the registration card.

'I've forgotten to fill in that card you gave me. Can I let you have it the next time I come?' he offered, pausing by the reception desk. Lucy didn't stop to wait for him and he saw the young woman frown as she watched her hurrying away.

'Yes, if Miss Adams is with you to authorise it,' she agreed, guardedly. 'We have a strict rule that either a parent or a guardian must be present whenever anyone's name is added to the register. It saves any confusion about who can and can't remove a child from the crèche.'

'I understand,' he said grimly because he didn't like being made to feel as though he was doing something wrong by wanting to see his own daughter.

He left the crèche and followed Lucy across the foyer, finally catching up with her as she was about to leave the building. It was pouring down with rain and he could see the problem she was having, trying to open her umbrella while holding onto Izzy.

'Here, let me hold her while you do that,' he offered, reaching out to take the baby from her.

'I can manage,' she snapped, moving Izzy out of his reach.

Connor swore under his breath. He was fast reaching the end of his patience. 'I was only offering to hold her. I wasn't trying to abduct her, although it might not be such a bad idea. The poor kid will be a nervous wreck if you react like that every time I go near her.'

'Then maybe you should leave us alone.' She'd finally

managed to open the umbrella and she glared at him as she moved off the step. 'Izzy and I don't need your help. We can manage perfectly well on our own.'

'You really think so?' He followed her across the car park, his mood not improved by the fact that he was getting soaked. The temperature in Boston had been in the high eighties when he'd left so he'd never thought to pack a raincoat. It was with the rest of his belongings that were waiting to be shipped over to England. 'You honestly think you can be both a mother and a father to her, do you?'

'Yes!' She glared at him as she stopped beside an elderly Ford Fiesta and unlocked the door. 'So if you came here full of noble intentions about taking care of us, you can forget them, Connor. I don't want you interfering in Izzy's life. I'm perfectly capable of looking after her all by myself!'

'Maybe you are, but what you want isn't the issue,' he replied tersely, wondering how they'd reached this point so quickly. Even though he'd been furious with her for cutting him out of his daughter's life, he'd sworn he would handle the situation calmly and with diplomacy. However, all his good intentions had disappeared when he'd heard her making those less-than-flattering remarks about him earlier in the day.

'It's what's best for Izzy that matters, not your feelings or mine. She's the important one in all of this, the one who stands to get hurt if you refuse to see sense.' There was a definite bite in his voice now. It was galling to realise that he'd been upset by what she'd said. He'd always believed that he was inured against other people's opinions, but Lucy's opinion of him seemed to matter an awful lot.

'It's Izzy I'm thinking about,' she retorted, bending down

to strap the baby into the car seat and obviously forgetting that she still had hold of the umbrella.

Connor sighed when a shower of rainwater cascaded over him. 'Why don't you give me that before you do some real damage with it? Even *you* can't manage to hold an umbrella *and* strap a baby into that seat.'

Her brown eyes flashed as he took the umbrella out of her hand but she must have decided it was easier not to argue with him. Connor held the umbrella so that it shielded her from the rain while she strapped Izzy into the seat. He handed it back to her once she'd finished, one dark brow arching when she grudgingly thanked him.

'See? It wasn't that difficult to do what I suggested, was it?'

'Meaning that I should always follow your suggestions? I don't think so.'

She opened the driver's door but he put out his hand as she went to get into the car. 'Why not, if they make sense? Or are you so determined to pay me back for wanting to get to know my own child that you'd do anything to spite me?'

'I don't give a damn about you, Connor! I'm not interested in paying you back or being spiteful. The only person I care about is Izzy and I won't have you breaking her heart!'

'Breaking her heart?' he repeated, knowing that he must sound as shocked as he felt. He gripped hold of the door when she tried to wrench it out of his grasp. 'You're not going any-where until you explain what you meant by that. Why on earth would I want to break my own daughter's heart?'

'Because it's what will happen if she gets in the way of your precious career. Oh, you might think that you want to play the doting father at the moment, but what's going to happen in a few months' time when you realise that having a child means having a lot of extra responsibilities? Which will come first then, Connor—your career or your daughter?'

'That's ridiculous,' he protested, but she didn't allow him to finish.

'No, it's the truth. Everything you do is geared to one thing and one thing only: your career. You don't have time for anything else, so do you really think it's fair to upset Izzy's life on a whim?'

'It isn't a whim! And I have no intention of upsetting her life. I plan on being a proper father to her and nothing you can say will make me change my mind about that.'

He glanced round as a car further along the row started up. There were a lot of staff leaving at the end of their shifts and he realised they couldn't continue the discussion when they might be overheard. He had no intention of trying to hide the fact that he was Izzy's father, but they needed to sort this out in private, although any hopes he'd had of reaching an agreement with Lucy were rapidly disappearing.

'We need to talk about this and we can't do it here,' he said bluntly, trying not to think about what had led her to have such a low opinion of him. He'd always prided himself on his honesty and had never made any secret of the fact that he hadn't been looking for commitment so why was she behaving as though he'd let her down?

He hurried on because he didn't know how to deal with all these new and strange emotions that kept assailing him. 'What time does Izzy go to bed?'

'I don't have time to talk to you tonight or any other night, for that matter,' she declared, but he was in no mood to placate her.

'Then I suggest you make time, because I'm not prepared

to wait until you decide that you do feel like talking to me.'
He stared back at her, feeling his heart ache when he saw the
fear that flickered in her soft brown eyes.

'She usually goes to bed at seven. Leave it until after then
so you don't upset her routine.'

'Let's make it seven-thirty,' he said gruffly, feeling like a
heel for scaring her. 'Are you still living in the same place?'

'No. I moved out of there before Izzy was born.'

She told him her new address then got into the car. Connor
didn't say anything else as she closed the door. Apologising
would have put him in a very vulnerable position and she had
to believe that he was serious about this or she would do her
best to cut him out of Izzy's life.

It was still pouring down with rain as he walked back
across the car park and the weather seemed to mirror his de-
jection at the way things had gone. He'd handled the situation very badly and he would have to try a lot harder in the
future if he wasn't going to alienate Lucy.

He sighed. Despite what he'd told her, he didn't want to
have to resort to a messy court hearing to gain access to Izzy.
He would much prefer it if they could reach an agreement by
themselves although if he couldn't make Lucy see sense, he
might not have any option except to apply to the courts.

The thought of the heartache that would cause was very
hard to deal with. His spirits had sunk to an all-time low by
the time he reached the paediatric unit. He could barely raise
a smile when he met Bea Francis in the corridor and saw her
surprise at his bedraggled state.

'I'd forgotten about the joys of a British summer.'

'So it would appear.' She grinned at him. 'So much for

Lucy's theory that you came back because you were missing our glorious weather!'

Connor drummed up a smile but it hurt to know that Lucy preferred to joke about the reason for his return rather than admit the truth. She was determined that no one would find out that he was Izzy's father and he knew how difficult it was going to be to change her mind. It was a relief when Bea asked him if he'd take a look a Sophie Fisher because it was easier to focus on work than his own problems.

He quickly changed into a clean set of scrubs then made his way to the high-dependency unit. Dee was there and he could tell immediately that she wasn't happy about the little girl's condition. He checked the ECG tracing and understood immediately why she was so concerned. Sophie was exhibiting clear signs of ventricular fibrillation—rapid, uncoordinated and ineffective heart contractions. It was a common complication of myocardial infarction and although it could be successfully resolved by the use of drugs in many cases, the drugs weren't working in this instance.

'She'll need cardioversion. I can do it here but I need to inform her parents first about what's happening.'

'They're in the relatives' room,' Dee told him.

'I'll have a word with them and come straight back.'

Connor left the room and went to find the child's parents. He waved them back to their seats and pulled up a chair, knowing how difficult this would be for them. 'My name is Connor Mackenzie and I'm the new head of the paediatric unit,' he told them, keeping the introductions brief. 'I'm afraid that Sophie isn't responding as well as we'd hoped she would to the drugs that were meant to settle her heart back into its proper rhythm.'

'So what's going to happen?' Mrs Fisher asked anxiously.

'I'll have to perform cardioversion to restore her heart's natural rhythm.'

'Cardioversion? I'm sorry, Dr Mackenzie, but you've lost me.' Mr Fisher leant forward in his seat and Connor could see the fear in his eyes. 'It's not another operation, is it? Sophie was fine until they took her to that theatre.'

'No, it's not an operation and we'll be able to do it right here in the high-dependency unit.'

He smiled reassuringly, thinking about all the times he'd been in this position. Reassuring parents was all part of his job and he'd always prided himself on his caring yet straight-forward approach. However, he'd never fully appreciated before how stressful it must be for them to have to entrust their child to a stranger. All of a sudden, it was as though he could *feel* the Fishers' fear, and it shocked him that he could empa-thise with them to such an extent.

'It's quite a simple procedure. I'll administer a brief electric shock to Sophie's heart. It's done by placing two special metal paddles on the chest wall, one below her right clavicle—her collar-bone—and the other just about here…' he pointed to his own chest '…over the cardiac apex. The sudden burst of electricity should restore her heart's natural rhythm.'

'And you're sure it will work?' Mrs Fisher asked desper-ately. 'Sophie will be all right, won't she?'

'I'm very hopeful about the outcome,' Connor said gently, wishing he could give the poor woman a cast-iron guarantee. It simply wasn't possible to do that so he smiled at the couple as he stood up. 'I'll come back to see you as soon as it's over, so try not to worry too much.'

It was the same advice he'd given to hundreds of parents

over the years but as he made his way back to the high-dependency unit, he found himself wondering how *he* would react if Izzy was about to undergo the procedure. It didn't bear thinking about, and it made him see that his life as he'd known it had changed for ever. Now that he had a child of his own, he would find it far more difficult to keep a rein on his emotions.

Just for a moment, he found himself wondering if he'd been right to come back to Dalverston to claim his daughter. What if he couldn't handle the responsibility of being a parent, as Lucy had said? He didn't want to hurt Izzy—it was the last thing he wanted to do! But how could he be sure that he would be a good father to Izzy when he had no real experience of what a parent was supposed to do? What if all his good intentions weren't enough, and he ended up making a mess of things?

Connor took a deep breath. This was neither the time nor the place to worry about that. Right now he had to concentrate on what he did best—and save a child's life.

It was well past seven before Lucy managed to get Izzy to sleep. Normally she had no problem settling the little girl down for the night but the change to her daily routine had obviously unsettled her.

She tiptoed from the bedroom, sighing when she saw all the toys that were strewn around the sitting-room. It had been a mad dash to get ready that morning for work. She had been intending to clear up as soon as she'd got home but she'd not had a chance because Izzy had been so fretful. However, she certainly didn't want Connor to see the flat in this state or he really would think that she couldn't cope!

She had just started to clear up the toys when the doorbell rang and she groaned. It was typical bad luck that he should be early when she'd wanted to be all prepared before he arrived. She went to let him in, trying to ignore the jolt her heart gave when he brushed against her as he stepped into the hall. Allowing herself to think of Connor as anything more than a threat would be a big mistake.

'You're early,' she said sharply, leading the way into the sitting-room.

'Am I?' He checked his watch and shrugged. 'What's five minutes between friends?'

Lucy forbore to say anything but if he'd been trying to goad her by that comment, he'd succeeded. They weren't friends and never would be now! Her heart suddenly lurched and she quickly battened it down. It wouldn't help to start remembering what they had been once upon a time.

'It looks like a tornado has hit this place.' He smiled as he looked around the room. 'You were always such a neat freak, too, Lucy. You used to get all uptight if I left anything out of place when I stayed overnight.'

'Did I? I'm afraid I don't remember.'

She bent down and quickly gathered up a handful of building blocks, refusing to be drawn into a discussion about the past. It didn't matter what had happened then because it was all over and done with. She and Connor no longer shared their lives. The only link between them now was Izzy and if she had her way, it was a link that would be severed as soon as possible.

'Don't you? How strange.' He crouched down beside her and picked up a stuffed rabbit which had one eye missing. He tossed it into the toy box then glanced at her. 'I remember it all, Lucy, all the fun we had, all the laughter…everything.'

'Then your memory must be better than mine obviously is.'

She stood up abruptly, unsure why he was going down this route. Did he think that he could *soften* her up by telling her that he remembered the time they'd spent together? They had gone out together for six months and it had been a happy time, too, probably the best time in her entire life. But if it had really meant anything to him then he would never have left her, would he?

The thought brought a rush of emotions with it and she turned away, terrified that he would see how vulnerable she felt. She'd tried her best to get over him so she could make a life for herself and Izzy, but there was no point pretending that he didn't still have the power to affect her.

'I'll make some coffee,' she said, heading towards the tiny kitchen.

'That would be great. Thanks.'

Lucy went into the kitchen and filled the kettle then stood there while the water boiled. She couldn't face going back until she had herself under control again. Connor might be making an effort to appear friendly but she mustn't be fooled into thinking that it meant he would give up his quest to play a part in Izzy's life. Once he made up his mind, he rarely changed it, so all she could do now was to protect her daughter the best way she could. He wasn't going to break Izzy's heart as he had broken hers.

CHAPTER FOUR

'THANKS.'

Connor took the mug of coffee that Lucy offered him and sat down. Now that the time had come to talk, he wasn't sure how to begin. He didn't want to antagonise her, but he needed to make it clear that he was determined to play an active part in Izzy's life—with or without her consent. Her main objection seemed to stem from the fear that he would grow tired of the responsibility of being a father, so maybe he should try to reassure that he had given the situation a lot of careful thought.

'I know it must have been a shock for you when I turned up today,' he said, easing himself into the conversation. 'With the benefit of hindsight, I can see that I should have got in touch with you before I left Boston.'

'It would have been less stressful for both of us if you had done,' she said coolly, sitting down.

Connor might have believed that she was completely in control of herself if he hadn't noticed the way her hands trembled as she lifted the cup of coffee to her lips. His heart contracted when he realised that her composure was merely a façade. Inside, Lucy was terrified about what was happening and he hated having to put her through such an ordeal. But he didn't have a choice. He intended to be there for Izzy, no matter what it cost him or Lucy to achieve his objective.

'It would. And I can only apologise that I didn't realise it sooner.' He shrugged. It wouldn't help his case if he let her see how nervous he felt, too. 'However, what's done is done and there's no point sitting here bewailing the fact. What we have to decide now is which way we're going to handle this. I suppose it's a case of sorting out the logistics.'

'Logistics?' Lucy put her cup on the table and stared at him. 'I'm not sure what you mean by that.'

'Obviously, we need to work out a rota for when I can see Izzy. And when she gets a bit older then we'll have to decide how often she can stay with me—'

'Stay with you!' She leapt to her feet and he saw all the colour drain from her face. 'You really think that I'm just going to hand her over to you?'

'Of course not. But there is no reason why she can't stay with me, is there?' Connor deliberately moderated his tone. They would get nowhere if they kept arguing and he had to do all he could to keep things calm. However, it seemed that Lucy had other ideas as she rounded on him.

'There is no *way* that I am allowing Izzy to stay with you! Quite apart from the fact that she doesn't even know you, I don't trust you to take proper care of her!'

'I'm her father. And I think that gives me certain rights, including the right to look after her,' he snapped, stung by the comment. 'Izzy won't come to any harm when she's with me and I resent you suggesting that she will.'

'And what happens if there's some sort of emergency at

work while you're looking after her? What do you propose to do then? Phone up the hospital and say that you're very sorry but you can't respond? I don't think so, do you?'

She laughed scornfully, the colour rushing back to her face as quickly as it had left it. Connor felt his pulse leap as it struck him how beautiful she looked with her eyes ablaze and her cheeks all rosy like that. She had always possessed a delicate beauty which had never failed to stir him, but this new, feisty Lucy was even more beguiling. It was an effort to drive the thought from his mind but he needed to focus on more important issues now.

'If I was taking care of Izzy then obviously I would have to make provision if I was called out. I wouldn't just abandon her, if that's what you're suggesting.'

'And I'm supposed to be happy with that, am I? You would, quote, *make provision* for her? Well, I'm sorry, Connor, but that's just not good enough. Izzy isn't a parcel that you can hand over to someone else whenever you choose. She needs people who will always be there for her, and not just when it's convenient. Looking after a child means putting them first and everything else second, and I just don't think you're capable of doing that.'

'You have no idea what I'm capable of!' He stood up as well, incensed by her refusal to believe him. Maybe he hadn't explained things very well but there was no question of him treating Izzy like a parcel!

'That's where you're wrong. I know exactly what you're like. We were together for six months, don't forget, and not once during that time did you let anything come before your job.'

She didn't back down and it was the fact that she wasn't prepared to meet him halfway that hurt most of all. Lucy must have a really poor opinion of him if she wouldn't accept that he truly cared about his own daughter.

'Maybe I didn't, but that was then and this is now.' His tone was harsh but it was the only way he knew how to hide this pain he was feeling. The fact that Lucy didn't consider him fit to take care of their child hurt unbearably.

'Meaning that I would always have come second to your job?'

The hurt in her voice was almost his undoing. Connor longed to tell her that it wasn't true, but it would have been a lie. His job had always come first and there was no point wishing that he'd done things differently now. However, Lucy had no idea how hard it had been to stick to the decision he'd made to concentrate exclusively on his career while they had been together.

'If you want to put it that way then, yes, I suppose you could say that. I never made any secret of the fact that I was ambitious, did I, Lucy?'

'No, you certainly didn't.' She gave a brittle laugh as she sat down. 'I have to give you full marks for honesty, Connor. I was never in any doubt that our relationship had an expiry date stamped on it.'

He wasn't sure if he liked that assessment of his actions but it seemed pointless to argue about it. He sat down and picked up his cup, giving himself a breathing space while he tried to decide what to do. He needed to convince Lucy that he could be trusted to look after Izzy and it wasn't going to be an easy task from the look of it.

'Look, Connor, we can argue about this all night but you aren't going to change my mind. I am prepared to let you see Izzy but that's all. There is no way that I will allow her to stay with you. For heaven's sake, I don't even know where you live!'

'I've rented a flat in that new complex near the business park. It wouldn't have been my first choice because it's too far from the hospital, but it was the best I could find at short notice.'

'I know where you mean. I looked at one of those flats myself but it was too expensive for me. Mum and Dad offered to help me with the rent but it wouldn't have been fair to expect them to subsidise me. Dad's hoping to retire this year and they'll need every penny.'

'Why did you decide to move out of your old flat?' he asked, feeling the same ambivalence he'd always felt whenever she'd spoken about her family. He knew how close Lucy was to her parents and her two older sisters, although he had never met them. He had deliberately kept his distance and had refused whenever she'd invited him to any family functions. Getting to know her family would have made it that much harder for her when they'd parted, and he'd wanted to protect her as much as he could. Or that had been what he'd told himself.

Now he found himself wondering if he'd really been protecting himself. Lucy had always had a hold over him, and he'd realised at the start of their relationship how dangerous it would be to get too deeply involved with her.

'It all came down to money again. The rent was just too much for me once I left work. Added to that, the lift kept breaking down all the time. It would have been a nightmare trying to drag a pram up all those stairs.'

'I never thought about that,' he said softly, trying not to dwell on the thought of his own vulnerability. He'd made a vow many years ago that he would live his life the way he chose to live it, but now he could see that a lot of the decisions he'd made in the last year had been influenced by Lucy.

It was an effort to focus on what she had said and he frowned because it was the second time she'd mentioned that she hadn't been able to afford the rent. He couldn't help feeling guilty at the thought of her struggling to pay her way while she'd been expecting their child.

'You don't think about it until you find yourself six months pregnant and standing at the bottom of four flights of stairs.' She suddenly laughed. 'It's a good job I moved out before I got any bigger. It would have needed a crane to get me up all those stairs by the time I was due to have Izzy. I was absolutely huge!'

'I don't believe you were *that* big,' Connor protested.

'Believe me, I was. There wasn't much to choose between me and a baby elephant. You should have seen me!'

'I wish I had.'

Connor felt the blood rush to his head when he realised what he'd said. It was the last thing he should have admitted in the circumstances. He needed to maintain a certain distance between them if this was to work, yet now that he'd come this far, he couldn't seem to stop.

'I would have loved to watch our baby growing inside you, Lucy,' he said, his voice grating with the sheer force of his feelings. 'It would have been the most wonderful experience of my life.'

Lucy felt her heart catch. There was something in Connor's voice that made her want to believe that he really meant that. Just for a moment she allowed herself to imagine what might have happened if he'd stayed in England while she'd been having Isabel.

He would have been with her when she'd had her first

scan, and been there, too, when she'd felt the baby start to move. He would have been with her when she'd gone to the antenatal classes and helped her with her breathing exercises.

Then there would have been the birth—the long, pain-filled hours when she'd laboured to bring their child into the world. It would have been so much easier if he'd been there, encouraging her and soothing her.

After Izzy was born, everything would have been different, too. He could have shared the night-time feeds with her, taken Izzy out in her pram, done all the things a proud new father was supposed to do. He had missed out on such a lot—*she* had missed out on such a lot—but it had been his decision to leave. She hadn't sent him away—he had chosen to go because he hadn't cared enough about her to stay. She must never let herself forget that, and definitely mustn't allow herself to be seduced by the thought of what might have been.

'I'm sure the reality would have been a lot less appealing. Anyway, I doubt you came here tonight to hear about my pregnancy, Connor. The only thing we need to decide is how much input you are to have in Izzy's life.'

She tossed back her hair, refusing to let him see how difficult it was for her to behave so coldly towards him. Connor had always aroused her very strongest emotions and it was hard to treat him with indifference but she couldn't afford to weaken. She had to stay strong for Izzy's sake.

'Obviously, I want to see her as often as I can.'

His tone was clipped and Lucy shot him a wary glance but it was impossible to tell what he was thinking. She bit back a sigh. He had always been a master at hiding his feelings, as she knew from experience.

'Then maybe you could come round on Sunday and see her

for an hour or so then. I'm working set days at the moment and I have every weekend off so Sunday would be the best day for me.'

'I'm afraid that isn't good enough, Lucy. I want to spend some real time with Izzy, not just an hour or so every weekend. She's never going to get to know me properly at that rate.'

'Well, *I'm* afraid it's all I'm prepared to offer you. I have no intention of allowing you to disrupt Izzy's life. She needs stability more than anything else and I certainly don't want her getting attached to you when, in a couple of months' time, you'll probably be sick and tired of playing the doting father.'

'How many more times do I have to tell you that it isn't going to happen? I am not going to disappear from Izzy's life. I intend to stick around until she's grown up, whether you like it or not.'

'I hear what you're saying, Connor, but I don't believe you. Nothing has ever come before your precious career and nothing ever will. I will not allow you to hurt Izzy the way you hurt—'

She broke off when she realised what she'd been about to say. Letting Connor know how vulnerable she was would be a mistake when it could have repercussions for her daughter.

'I didn't come here to fight with you, Lucy.' He stood up and his green eyes were hooded when he looked at her. 'I also didn't come here to upset you and I apologise if that's what I've done. This situation is difficult enough without us falling out all the time.'

'I don't want to argue with you either. My only concern is to protect Izzy,' she said quietly, surprised that he hadn't tried to use her unwitting slip to his own advantage.

'Izzy is my only concern, too.'

He spread his hands wide open in a gesture that smacked of defeat and it was such a shock to see it that she didn't know what to say. Connor Mackenzie and defeat were two concepts that shouldn't be aired in the same breath, yet she could see for herself how desperate he was to convince her.

'Why, Connor?' Maybe it was that thought which unlocked her tongue, but all of a sudden she knew that she needed to understand his motives better. 'You never mentioned that you wanted a family when we were together so I can't understand why you are so keen to be a father to Izzy. It just doesn't fit with everything I know about you.'

'Maybe it doesn't fit, but I'm serious about this, Lucy. I don't want Izzy growing up thinking that I don't care about her. I do care. I care very much and I shall do everything in my power to play an active role in her life, too.'

His tone was uncompromising yet she saw the flicker of pain in his eyes and realised there was more to that statement than just a desire not to be thwarted. Something had driven him to come back to England to claim his daughter and she only wished that she knew what it was. However, even though she knew that he was serious about his intentions, she still didn't trust him. If it came to a choice between his job and Izzy, which would he choose?

It was that uncertainty which made Lucy hold back, that plus the fear of what would happen if she allowed him back into her life. She still loved him, still felt the same attraction for him, so how could she be sure that she was doing what was right for Izzy? She couldn't bear to think that Izzy could get hurt because she'd been influenced by her feelings for him.

'I've offered to let you see Izzy on Sunday. If that isn't enough, then I'm sorry but there is nothing more I can do. My offer still stands, Connor, and it's up to you to decide if you want to accept it.'

'I could go to the court and apply for an access order,' he said menacingly.

'I'm sure you could. You'd probably get it too…eventually. However, are you really prepared to go to such lengths when I will stop you having any contact with Izzy in the interim?'

'Is that a threat?'

'Yes. But it's no more of a threat than you just made towards me.' She stood up abruptly, wanting to bring the discussion to an end because she'd had enough for one day. 'I will not be bullied into doing what you want, Connor. My only concern is Izzy and what is best for her.'

'I am *not* trying to bully you. I'm trying to make you see sense!' He gripped her arms. 'Izzy needs both her mother and her father in her life—can't you understand that?'

'No, I can't!' She glared up at him as all the emotions she'd experienced that day suddenly spilled over. 'So far as I'm concerned, Izzy would be better off with just one parent than having you as her father!'

She knew she'd gone too far when she saw his face close up. She was already trying to free herself when he hauled her towards him. Lucy knew he was going to kiss her and her eyes filled with tears at the thought. The last thing she wanted was for him to kiss her in anger when it would ruin all the precious memories she'd clung to these past, lonely months.

And yet when his mouth found hers there was no hint of anger in the warm, hard feel of his lips, no sense at all that he was trying to punish her. Connor was kissing her as though he needed this kiss just to survive; he was kissing her with a depth of emotion that shocked her when she couldn't recall him ever kissing her like that before.

Her lips softened, clung to his as she felt the rawness of

their passion explode around them. The kiss seemed to go on and on even though she knew it could have lasted for only a few seconds. When he pushed her away, he was breathing heavily, but so was she. The kiss had unleashed a lot of emotions in both of them and she had no idea what was going to happen now.

He spun round on his heel and a moment later she heard the front door slam. The noise must have woken Izzy because she began to cry. Lucy dragged some air into her depleted lungs as she made her way to the bedroom and lifted Izzy out of her cot. The little girl was hot and fretful so she took her into the kitchen and gave her a drink, and all the time she was attending to her needs, Lucy's mind kept spinning in circles. Why had Connor kissed her like that? What did it mean?

She had no idea what the answers were, but it scared her to know that he still wanted her. If he'd been indifferent to her, she could have coped, but each time she saw him now she would remember how his mouth had felt—hungry and tender—and it would be that much harder to do what was right for Izzy.

Tears filled her eyes again at the thought that her child might get hurt because of her. She had to remember that it wasn't her feelings that mattered or Connor's, but this precious child's, the child who had been born as a result of their passion for each other. She mustn't allow their passion to hurt her now.

Connor spent a sleepless night. Jet-lag was still playing havoc with his internal clock but he knew it wasn't the time difference that was to blame. It was what had happened in Lucy's flat that plagued him most of all.

He got up before the sun had risen over the surrounding

hills and stood by the kitchen window, nursing a cup of black coffee. He could tell himself a thousand times that it had been anger that had driven him to kiss her and it would be true to a point. But beyond that point had come a moment when passion had taken over: his passion for her; her passion for him.

He had wanted Lucy so much last night that even now his body ached for her. As soon as he'd taken her in his arms, he'd been beset by the familiar feel of her soft curves, the scent of her hair, the softness of her skin. It was as though everything that made Lucy who she was had been imprinted in his mind and all it had taken had been that first touch to push all the right buttons. If he hadn't left when he had then he knew what would have happened, and it was the last thing he needed at the moment. Making love with Lucy would complicate matters far too much!

He emptied the coffee down the drain and went into the bathroom to take a shower. He wouldn't achieve anything by brooding about what had happened last night. He had to forget about it and focus on what really mattered, which was Izzy. Lucy seemed determined to keep him on the fringes of their daughter's life and he was equally determined that she wasn't going to succeed. If he kept that thought at the forefront of his mind then he might have a hope of winning this particular battle.

The paediatric unit was bustling when he arrived shortly after six a.m. He could see the surprise on the nursing staff's faces as he bade them a brisk good morning. His predecessor had been no sluggard but it was unheard of for the head of the department to appear at such an early hour. Bea was obviously shocked to see him and made no bones about it either.

'I hope this isn't going to become a habit. The nursing staff will start to revolt if you're here at this time every morning, checking up on them.'

'I'm not checking up on anyone. I just couldn't sleep so I decided to avoid the rush hour and come in early,' he explained, not wanting his staff to get the wrong impression, although it was a good job that Lucy hadn't arrived yet because she certainly wouldn't have believed him. She seemed determined to think the worst of him…apart from when he kissed her, of course. She hadn't seemed to have had too many objections then!

The thought did nothing to soothe him so he drove it out of his mind. 'How's Sophie Fisher doing?'

'Much better than she was.'

Bea seemed to have been mollified by his explanation so he chalked it up as one small success as she accompanied him to the high-dependency unit. 'The cardioversion did the trick and she seems to have settled down now. Dee insisted on staying with her so she's still here. I have to say that Dee's been an absolute godsend. We had a bit of a rush through the night—an RTA plus a perforated appendix—and we couldn't have managed without her. I don't suppose you could use your legendary charm to persuade her to stay?'

Connor laughed. 'I can try, although I'm a bit short on charm at the moment, I should warn you. It must be the jet-lag.'

Bea rolled her eyes. 'I'm sure you're being far too modest. Just give it your best shot.'

Connor let himself into the room as Bea hurried away. Dee was sitting by the bed and he waved her back to her seat when she went to get up. 'Stay where you are. From what Bea's been telling me, you've done more than your share through the night.'

Dee smiled tiredly. 'I just did what I could to help.'

'Well, it was greatly appreciated. In fact, Bea asked me if I would try to persuade you to stay on,' he told her, taking the chart off the end of the bed and glancing through the meticulously maintained notes.

'It's nice to know I'm appreciated but I don't think I could cope with a full-time job at the moment. I need to get my head round what's happened.'

'I understand. But if you feel like doing a few hours then just say the word. It might help if you took your mind off your problems for a while.'

Connor hung the chart back in its place. Sophie's condition had improved tremendously and he was delighted with her progress. He would be able to move her onto the ward later that day which would ease the staffing problem, although it didn't mean that he intended to allow the present situation to continue. The high-dependency unit needed to be available twenty-four seven and not just when they could find someone to man it.

'I wish.' Dee gave him a watery smile as she stood up. 'If I could make my problems disappear that easily then I'd sign up like a shot, but this problem isn't going to go away. I'm never going to have a child of my own now and it isn't fair to Mike to expect him to marry me when it means he's never going to be a father.'

Connor sighed when he saw tears start to run down Dee's face. He had worked with her fiancé, Mike Wilson, in Boston and had a lot of respect for him. He knew how gutted Mike had been when they had found out that the treatment Dee had received for an aggressive form of childhood cancer had left her infertile. Maybe it was the fact that he had just discovered that he had a child of his own which had made their situation so

poignant, but when Mike had asked him if he would look after
Dee on the journey back to England, Connor had agreed at once.

Normally, he was wary of getting involved in other people's affairs, but making sure that Dee got home safely to her
family, who lived outside Dalverston, had seemed the least he
could do in the circumstances. That should have been the end
of his involvement, but he couldn't help being moved when
he saw the misery on her face.

He made his way around the bed and put his arm round her.
'It will all work out in the end, Dee. You'll see.'

'I don't see how it can. Mike's never made any secret of
the fact that he wants kids, and I can't have them…!'

Connor sighed as she put her head on his shoulder and
began to sob. He was just wondering what else he could say
to comfort her when the door opened and Bea poked her head
into the room. Connor saw the start the ward sister gave when
she saw him and Dee, and knew immediately how it must have
appeared. They must have looked like two lovers, standing
there entwined in each other's arms, and the thought made
him want to gnash his teeth in frustration.

He knew what the hospital grapevine was like and dreaded
to think what Lucy was going to say when she found out that
he and Dee had been caught in such circumstances. It certainly
wasn't going to improve his standing in her eyes, and his
heart sank at the thought of the problems it could cause.

It seemed that a bad situation was about to get worse.

CHAPTER FIVE

'APPARENTLY, they were all over each other like a rash. I thought there was something going on, didn't you, Lucy?'

'Didn't I what?' Lucy shoved her coat into her locker and slammed the door. Izzy had been very clingy when she'd taken her to the crèche that morning and it had been hard to leave her. She'd waited outside until she'd been sure that Izzy had settled down then had had to rush so as not to be late for the changeover. She hadn't really been listening to what Sandra had been saying.

'Connor and Dee, of course.' Sandra sighed when Lucy looked blankly at her. 'You didn't hear a word that I said, did you?'

'Sorry. I was miles away.'

'Bea caught Connor and Dee *at it* in the high-dependency unit!'

'At it?'

'Yes, you know—making out, kissing and canoodling, and all the other euphemisms your mum used to come up with.' Sandra pulled a face. 'Looks as though I'm wasting my time lusting after the gorgeous Connor. It's just my luck, too.

Whenever I set my sights on a guy, someone else always gets there ahead of me!'

'I...um...I'll have to go. I need to see Bea so I'll catch up with you later.'

Lucy hurried out of the staffroom before Sandra could see how devastated she felt by the news. Connor had been caught kissing Dee? Could it be true?

A wave of sickness rushed up her throat and she had to stop before she went into the office. She wasn't sure why she was so shocked when she'd suspected that there'd been something going on between them. However, the thought of Connor and the other woman made her feel ill after what had happened last night.

She'd honestly thought that he'd felt the same as she had done about that kiss, but obviously not. It hadn't been passion that had driven him to kiss her that way but a desire to make her bend to his will. Well, if that was the case then he was in for a shock because nobody, not even the wonderful Connor Mackenzie, was going to manipulate her like that!

She opened the office door, summoning a smile when Bea glanced up. There was no way that she wanted anyone to know how hurt she felt. 'So what sort of a night did you have, then?'

'Hectic.' Bea yawned as she stood up. 'We had two emergency admissions, one straight after the other, so it was all systems go.'

'Just what you needed,' Lucy said sympathetically, picking up the nightly report sheet. She skimmed through the notes Bea had made, pausing when she came to the two new admissions. 'An RTA and a case of appendicitis?'

'That's right. Ben Roberts is the appendix. He's been a bit up and down since he woke up this morning so keep an eye on him, will you? Chloe Simmons is the RTA. She was thrown out of her father's car when it hit the central barrier on the motorway. Multiple fractures and a possible concussion, but she's stable so it could have been a lot worse.'

'What about her parents?' Lucy asked, hoping they weren't going to have to break any bad news to the child.

'Mum is upstairs in Women's Surgical with a broken pelvis but Dad is OK. Apparently, they were driving up to Scotland for their holidays and decided to travel through the night because the roads are quieter.' Bea sighed. 'The police think that the father fell asleep at the wheel.'

'It sounds likely.' Lucy skimmed through the rest of the notes but there was nothing unusual in them. She glanced up as Bea came round the desk. 'Off you go then and get your beauty sleep.'

'I wish! I have to ferry the kids to school first and then do some shopping before I go to bed.' Bea headed for the door then paused. 'Oh, before I forget, Connor is here. He arrived just after six and caused a real stir, too, although he promised he wouldn't make a habit of getting in so early. Anyway, he's in his office if you need him.'

'Right, thanks.'

Lucy sat down behind the desk, resisting the urge to ask Bea if the rumours were true. It had nothing to do with her what Connor did, although she was surprised that he had compromised his position by being caught in such a potentially embarrassing situation. He had always been a stickler about maintaining the proprieties when they'd been seeing each other, but then he hadn't wanted to run the risk of anyone finding out about their affair. Obviously his feelings for Dee were much deeper than his feelings had been for her if he was prepared to risk going public this time.

The thought hurt no matter how many times Lucy told herself it was silly to let it bother her. She tried not to think about it as she checked the diary to see which children were due to be discharged that morning then went into the ward. It was breakfast-time so she ushered those children who were allowed out of bed into the day-room then made sure that the others were eating. Daisy Banks, a five-year-old who'd had her badly infected tonsils removed two days earlier, started crying when Lucy tried to persuade her to eat some porridge.

'My throat hurts,' the little girl whimpered, pushing the bowl away.

'I know it does, sweetheart, but you won't get better if you don't eat anything.' Lucy gave her a cuddle then picked up the bowl. 'Do you like yoghurt? I think we have some pots in the fridge so maybe you could manage one of them instead.'

'Yes, please,' Daisy whispered, wiping her dripping nose on the back of her hand.

Lucy plucked a tissue out of the box and gave it to her then went to the ward kitchen. They kept a selection of simple foodstuffs in the fridge and she was relieved to see that there were a couple of pots of yoghurt left on the shelf.

She found a spoon then went back and gave it to Daisy, helping the child to tear off the lid. Once she was sure the little girl was eating it she checked on the other children. Ben Roberts, the boy who'd had his appendix removed, looked very listless when she stopped by his bed.

'Hi, Ben.' Lucy smiled at him as she took the thermometer out of its holder. 'I'm Staff Nurse Adams. I wasn't here when you were brought in last night so I'd like to check how you're doing. Can I take your temperature, please?'

Ben nodded so Lucy gently inserted the digital thermometer's probe into his ear. It gave an almost instantaneous reading and she frowned when she saw that Ben's temperature was higher than it should have been. She made a note on his chart then checked his pulse, her unease deepening when she discovered how rapid it was. It looked as though Ben might have an infection and it was something that needed to be dealt with as soon as possible.

She gave him a drink of water then went to the nursing station and phoned Connor's office number, feeling her heart kick in an extra beat when she heard his voice coming down the line. 'It's Staff Nurse Adams, Dr Mackenzie,' she said formally, deciding it would be easier if she used their professional status to maintain her distance. She didn't want to think about him and Dee after what had happened last night…

'I wonder if you could come and look at one of the children for me,' she said quickly, before she could get sidetracked.

'Of course. I'll be right down.'

He didn't ask her what was wrong with the child before he hung up and Lucy's lips snapped together. Was he feeling guilty about kissing her when he was having a relationship with another woman? She sincerely hoped so. Connor deserved to feel guilty after the way he'd behaved!

Connor could sense an atmosphere as soon as he went into the ward and sighed to himself. Obviously, Bea had told the others what she had seen, and they'd added two and two and come up with a hundred! He gritted his teeth when Sandra stalked past him with her nose in the air. Short of gathering the staff together and announcing that he and Dee weren't having an affair, there wasn't much he could do. Anyway, he'd be damned if he would explain himself. Let people think what they liked!

His resolve lasted just as long as it took to find Lucy and the minute he saw her expression, it started to waver. He couldn't bear to see the hurt in her eyes and know that he was responsible for putting it there.

'Look, Lucy, I don't know what you've heard—'

'Ben is in bed six, Dr Mackenzie. His temperature is a little higher than it should be so I thought you should take a look at him.'

She stepped around him, making it clear that she wasn't interested in what he had to say. Connor followed her into the ward, hating the fact that she'd made him feel as though he had done something wrong. He wasn't answerable to Lucy for his actions so why did he feel this way? Why did he *care* if she was hurt? His only concern was Izzy and he had to remember that.

Lucy handed him the boy's chart then waited while he read through it. From what he could see, everything had been fine when Ben had been admitted, but his temperature had started to rise in the last couple of hours. A perforated appendix often resulted in peritonitis—inflammation of the peritoneum, the membrane lining the abdominal cavity—and that could be extremely serious. He could understand why Lucy had wanted him to look at the child.

He hung the chart back on the bed and smiled at the boy. 'Hello, Ben. I'm Dr Mackenzie. How do you feel this morning?'

'I dunno. Sort of hot, and my tummy hurts…' The boy tailed off miserably and Connor nodded.

'Sounds as though I'd better take a look at you. I'm going to check the incision and feel all over your tummy so just yell out if it hurts.'

He put on some gloves while Lucy folded back the bedclothes, then carefully removed the dressing that had been placed over the incision. The surgeon had opted for the traditional method of removing an appendix by making an opening in the boy's abdomen large enough to perform the surgery. Opinion was divided about the benefits of minimally invasive, or keyhole, surgery when performing an appendectomy, and many surgeons still preferred the more conventional method.

Connor couldn't see anything wrong with the incision: the wound looked clean and there was no discharge from it. A plastic drainage tube had been inserted through a separate incision to drain off any pus and that too seemed to be fine. However, he frowned when he gently palpated Ben's abdomen. The muscles in the abdominal wall had gone into spasm, making it feel hard to the touch, and there was no sign of peristalsis—wave-like contractions of the intestinal muscles which were needed to pass food along the digestive tract. They were classic signs of peritonitis, which was something he would have hoped to avoid.

'Is there anything in the surgeon's report about an abscess around the appendix?' he asked, glancing at Lucy.

'I'll just check.' She opened the file she was holding and quickly read through the report. 'No, there's nothing here. It all seems quite straightforward, as you can see for yourself.'

Connor leant over so he could read the report over her shoulder. He realised his mistake as soon as he inhaled the familiar fragrance of her shampoo, but by that time it was too late to do anything about it. He just had to grit his teeth and pretend that he couldn't feel his body responding in time-honoured fashion.

'It all appears to have been very much routine,' he agreed shortly.

'Would you like me to phone the surgeon for you to check?' she suggested, glancing up at him.

'There's no need.'

Connor stepped back, knowing that he couldn't trust himself to remain that close to her for very much longer. Even now he could feel the memory of what had happened last night tugging at his senses and it was worrying to know how little control he had over his emotions. He should be thinking about Izzy, and how he was going to persuade Lucy to let him see more of her, instead of remembering how wonderful that kiss had been!

'What antibiotics has Ben been written up for?' he asked, determined to put an end to such nonsense. He nodded when Lucy told him the name and the quantity of the drug the attending surgeon had prescribed. 'That's fine, although I think I'll increase the dosage. I'd also like the lab to run some tests. We need to know exactly what we're dealing with and tailor the treatment accordingly.'

He wrote down his instructions and signed the lab sheet then turned to Ben and smiled. 'You should feel a bit better once the extra antibiotics start to kick in, but if your tummy gets any worse, you must tell one of the nurses immediately.'

'OK,' Ben promised, managing a smile this time.

Connor left the ward and went back to his office, sighing when he discovered that it was still only seven a.m. It felt as though he'd done a full day's work yet he still had many hours ahead of him. He had arranged to meet his new team at eight o'clock so he decided to get himself a cup of coffee then run through their personnel files before they arrived. It was important to understand his staff's strengths and weaknesses if they were to work together successfully.

He bought himself a large cup of coffee from the canteen and took it back to his desk then spent the next hour reading about the people he would be working with. There had been a lot of changes while he'd been away and both registrars were fairly new to the posts, but that wasn't a bad thing in his opinion. Although he had a deep respect for his predecessor, Connor had his own ideas about how things should be done and it would be easier to implement any changes if the staff weren't set in their ways. He had just finished when there was a knock on the door, heralding their arrival.

Connor invited them in and introduced himself. Martin Fellows, his senior registrar, seemed a very earnest type, while Amanda Dobson, his junior registrar, seemed far more relaxed. The final member of the team was Tom Bradshaw, a houseman who had just started a twelve-month rotation in the paediatric unit.

Once the pleasantries were over, Connor took them down to the ward. Although the personnel files had given him a background history on each member of the team, he wanted to see for himself how they fared with the patients. Lucy came out of the office to meet them, smiling politely as she bade him a formal good morning.

Connor knew it was unreasonable to expect anything more, but he couldn't help remembering how she used to behave around him. Even though she had been very discreet when they had been at work, she hadn't been able to hide the warmth in her eyes whenever she'd looked at him.

Lucy had really cared about him and that had been another reason why he'd left England. He hadn't wanted to risk breaking her heart, yet all of a sudden he found himself wishing that he could roll back the months. If he could have had that

time all over again then he was no longer sure if he would have
left her.

'This is Chloe Simmons. She was admitted last night following an RTA.'

Lucy handed the child's notes to Connor and moved aside
as he approached the bed. So far the ward round had gone like
clockwork and that was the way she intended it to continue.
So long as she treated him in a totally professional manner,
everything would be fine.

'No vomiting, I see. That's a good sign.' Connor skimmed
through the child's notes then turned to Tom Bradshaw. 'What
other symptoms might you expect to see in a classic case of
concussion, Tom?'

'Confusion, an inability to remember events immediately
prior to the injury, dizziness and blurred vision,' the junior
doctor rattled out on cue.

'And how long would you expect such symptoms to last?'
Connor continued.

'It depends on how long the person is unconscious. The
more prolonged the period of unconsciousness, the more
severe the symptoms tend to be, although I wouldn't want to
test out that theory,' Tom added. 'I'd want to find out sooner
rather than later if there was anything serious going on.'

'What do you mean by serious?' Connor queried.

'Extradural haemorrhage would be my main concern. If
there's bleeding between the skull and the brain then it would
need dealing with a.s.a.p.'

'Good. It's nice to know that some of the stuff you learned
in med school has sunk in.'

Lucy saw the relief on the younger man's face and hid her

smile. Obviously, Connor's reputation had gone before him. He gave so much of himself to the job that he never settled for less than one hundred per cent from the people he worked with. He also never made any allowance for the fact that they had private lives, as his team would soon discover. He lived and breathed his job, and it was a salutary reminder of how careful she needed to be about his involvement with Izzy. She wouldn't allow her daughter to become another casualty of Connor's over-developed work ethic.

The thought hummed away at the back of her mind as they finished the round. They were just about to leave the ward when Sandra came to tell them that there was a phone call from A and E for Connor so he went into the office to take it. Amanda Dobson staggered behind the desk and flopped down onto a chair as soon as he'd disappeared.

'Am I glad that's over! I couldn't sleep last night for worrying if he was going to be as bad as everyone said he would be. To hear people talk, you'd think he was Attila the Hun, but he was OK, really. What did you think, Martin?' she asked, glancing at the senior registrar.

'He seems to know his stuff all right,' Martin replied guardedly.

Amanda rolled her eyes. 'Of course he knows his stuff! He wouldn't have got the job otherwise. It's just that so many people have warned me how demanding he is that I'd built him up in my mind as some sort of a monster, but he was really nice, actually.'

'Maybe there's a reason why he's loosened up,' Tom suggested, grinning. 'They say that people act completely out of character when Cupid's arrow strikes, so that could explain it if the rumours are true.'

'What rumours?' Amanda demanded.

Lucy turned away as Tom launched into a lurid account of what had gone on that morning between Connor and Dee. She didn't want to listen to the story again when it would only remind her how stupid she'd been to imagine that last night's kiss had meant anything to him.

She went back into the ward and helped Daisy Banks's mother pack up her belongings. The little girl was being discharged that day so she explained to Mrs Banks that Daisy's throat would feel sore for a couple of weeks and that she should give her food that could be swallowed easily. She had just escorted them to the lift when Connor came to find her.

'A and E have a ten-year-old with suspected meningitis. I'm on my way there to see him so can you get one of the high-dependency beds ready? If it is meningitis then he will need monitoring very closely. Sophie Fisher can be moved onto the main ward. There's a bed free now that Daisy Banks has gone home.'

'Of course, but what are we going to do about staff? Dee's gone home and we can't expect her to come back when she worked all through last night.'

'I'll sort something out, but there's no way that I'm having that unit standing empty when we need to use the beds. I'll see if I can find someone to fill in on the ward while you cover in there, then ask Dee if she will do the night shift again.'

'Fine.'

Lucy didn't say anything else. Connor seemed to have it all worked out so who was she to argue, especially when she agreed with him that the unit should be open? It was a crime to have shut it when the beds were needed, although maybe Connor was so keen to use the facilities because it gave him the perfect excuse to have Dee around?

She sighed. Even if that was true, it had nothing to do with her. It was up to Connor what he did, although it would be different if his relationship with Dee had repercussions for Izzy, of course.

Lucy frowned. She had never given any thought to the implications it could have if Connor was involved with Dee, but maybe she should have done. If their affair really was serious then he was bound to have told Dee about Izzy and she wasn't sure how she felt about the other woman knowing that he was Izzy's father when she'd gone to such lengths to keep it a secret even from her own family.

Then there was the fact that he would want Dee to get to know Izzy—how did she feel about that? Could she stomach the thought of them playing happy families with her daughter?

Her heart sank when it struck her how complicated the situation was, and how little she could do about it. She could hardly issue Connor with an ultimatum and demand that he choose between his girlfriend and his daughter! She would have to wait and see what happened, but if she was at all concerned about the effect it was having on Izzy then she wouldn't hesitate to step in. She might not have a role in Connor's life any more, but she was Izzy's mother, and her main concern was to make sure that her daughter didn't get hurt.

CHAPTER SIX

'I'LL organise a lumbar puncture as soon as we get Alan into the high-dependency unit. In the meantime, I've started him on a course of intravenous antibiotics. Even though I can't be sure it is meningitis at this stage, I don't intend to take any chances.'

'How long is it going to take, Doctor?' The man checked his watch and sighed. 'I really could do without hanging around here for very much longer.'

'Alan will be moved to the paediatric unit within the next few minutes. Once he's been settled in, I'll do the lumbar puncture. We will then have to wait for the lab to send the results back to us.'

Connor didn't bother trying to be polite. Ten-year-old Alan Johnson lived in one of the local authority's care homes and it had soon become apparent that the care worker who had accompanied the boy to hospital was less than sympathetic to his plight.

'So it could be ages yet.' Graham White, the care worker, sounded extremely disgruntled by the news. 'I'm supposed to be off duty in half an hour's time, too.'

'Then I suggest you see if one of your colleagues can relieve you.' Connor walked away in disgust. Pity help the children in the home if all the carers adopted that attitude, he thought grimly as he went back into Resus.

It wasn't the first time he had encountered a situation like this, neither would it be the last. Normally, he didn't allow it to get to him but he couldn't seem to distance himself the way he used to. It was as though his emotions were simmering just beneath the surface, ready to erupt at the least provocation, and it was scary for a man like him who had always been in control before. It meant that he would have to be extra vigilant. He couldn't allow his new, more emotionally charged state to affect any decisions he made.

Once the transfer was organised, he went back upstairs. Lucy had moved Sophie out of the high-dependency unit and she was in the process of supervising a member of the hospital's cleaning staff when he arrived. Good hygiene practice was vital in a place like this, where the very sick were nursed, and he knew that he could rely on her to maintain the very highest standards. Her dedication was one of the things he had admired about her, although there had been many other things he'd found even more beguiling.

'How's it going?' He cut short that thought as she came out of the room. Remembering all the reasons why he'd been attracted to her wouldn't help, especially after last night.

'We're just about ready. Is it definitely meningitis?' she asked as they made their way to the office.

'I'd say so, although I'll need to do a lumbar puncture to confirm it. There's no stiffness in the neck, but the rest of the symptoms point towards it—photophobia, severe headache, fever and nausea.'

'Is there any sign of a rash?'

'Not yet, but there's what looks like a bruise in the crook of the boy's elbow. I've seen that happen before—first the bruise appears, then the rash develops later.' He shrugged. 'I've started him on intravenous antibiotics so they should help.'

'How did you get on about finding cover?' she queried, going over to the desk.

'The nursing officer has agreed to hire an agency nurse to cover your shifts for the rest of the week.'

'Really? I was told the powers that be had decided not to hire any more agency staff because of the extra costs it entails.' She suddenly laughed. 'You must have done some major arm-twisting to get a result like that!'

Connor smiled. 'Let's just say that I made it abundantly clear that I wouldn't accept any excuses.'

'I'll bet you did.' Her smile faded abruptly and he saw her face close up. 'Did you manage to get in touch with Dee about working tonight?'

'No, I haven't had time yet. I'll phone her later. If she can't come in then I'll have to twist a few more arms, I expect.'

He took a deep breath but even though she had rebuffed his earlier attempts to explain, he had to make it clear that the rumours about him and Dee weren't true. 'Dee and I are just friends, Lucy. I don't want you getting the wrong idea about us.'

'Your relationship with Dee has nothing to do with me,' she said briskly, taking a sheet of paper out of the tray. 'The lab report on Ben Roberts has come back. They've identified *Escherichia coli* as the source of the infection.'

'Not much of a surprise there, then. It's the most common of all the bacteria which cause peritonitis because it's always present in the intestine.'

Connor took the report from her, trying to hide his frustration at her continued refusal to listen to what he was trying to tell her. Either Lucy didn't want to believe that he wasn't involved with Dee, or she really didn't care.

His heart sank because the latter option seemed the most likely. He found it difficult to hide how much the idea upset him as he read through the lab's findings. 'At least it isn't MRSA so that's something to be thankful for,' he said, forcing himself to stick to the topic under discussion. 'I know Dalverston has an excellent reputation for infection control, but the number of cases of MRSA are increasing annually and we mustn't get complacent. The increased level of antibiotics will sort this out, but I'd like the nursing staff to keep a close eye on Ben until things have settled down.'

'Of course. I've put him down for extra obs so it isn't a problem,' she replied calmly, slipping the lab report back into the file, and the fact that she seemed able to function properly just seemed to prove how indifferent she was to him.

It made him wonder all of a sudden why she had kissed him with such passion the night before. Had it been a genuine response, or had she used his own passion to get back at him? It was a relief when Sandra knocked on the door to tell them their patient had arrived. He couldn't handle the thought that she might have been playing games with him.

They made their way to the high-dependency unit, pausing outside the door to spray their hands with a bactericidal cleanser. Everyone going into the unit was expected to take precautions to avoid cross-contamination and Connor could see that a notice to that effect had been pinned to the door. Lucy had thought of everything, it seemed, and it just confirmed his suspicions that she hadn't been swept away by the ardour of the moment. Lucy was far too organised to let herself get carried away.

He forced the thought to the very back of his mind as she handed him a disposable gown then took one off the shelf for herself. Once they were suitably attired, they went into the room. Alan appeared to be very drowsy—a common symptom of bacterial meningitis. He seemed to find it a huge effort to respond when Connor asked him how he was feeling.

'I don't know… My head hurts…thought the drugs would make it better.'

'They will, but they need time to kick in,' Connor assured him. 'You just need to be patient a little while longer.'

He glanced round as Lucy came back from drawing the blinds. Photophobia—an intolerance to light—was another symptom of meningitis and he could see the boy start to relax now that the room was in semi-darkness. He drew her aside so he could explain what he wanted to do.

'I'd like to get the lumbar puncture done as soon as possible. Can you get everything ready while I explain to Alan what's going to happen?'

'Do you want me to fetch his parents so they can be with him?'

'His parents aren't here,' he said, keeping a tight rein on his emotions. 'He lives in one of the local authority homes so he was brought here by a care worker. I'm not sure what's happened to the guy now—he's probably in the relatives' room.'

'Oh, I see.' She shot a sympathetic glance at the boy. 'I'll leave it for now, then. He can come and see Alan after we've finished.'

'That might be best.' Connor turned to the boy as she moved away, trying not to think about the sympathy he'd seen in her eyes just now. It wouldn't help him maintain the emotional balance he needed if he dwelt on it.

'Right, Alan, we have to find out exactly what is making

you so ill, so I'm going to do something called a lumbar puncture. All it means is that I'm going to take a little fluid from around your spinal cord.'

'Are you going to stick a needle in me?' the boy asked, looking scared to death.

'I'm afraid so, but it won't take long. And once I've managed to get some of the fluid I need for the tests, that will be it for now.'

'Promise?' Alan whispered fearfully.

'Cross my heart and hope to die!'

He made a cross over his heart, earning himself a wan smile for his efforts. Lucy had the tray all ready for him and she helped him roll the boy onto his side and place him in position with his chin tucked into his chest and his knees drawn up so that the vertebrae were drawn apart.

Connor quickly anaesthetised the skin over the lumbar spine with a little local anaesthetic then used a hollow needle inserted between the vertebrae to draw off some spinal fluid. Lucy covered the puncture site with a sterile dressing as soon as he'd finished, then they made the boy comfortable again.

'Well done! You were really brave,' Connor told him. 'That's the worst bit over so now I'm going to leave you to rest while the lab tests this sample. Staff Nurse Adams will be here if you need anything, and Mr White is still here if you'd like to see him.'

'No.' Alan closed his eyes. 'I don't want to see anyone from that place.'

'Then you just lie there and try to sleep.' Connor didn't say anything else as he left the room. He was afraid that anything he did say might be too revealing. Alan obviously wasn't happy in the care home and he understood why, too.

He knew from his own experiences what life was like for a child in care. You could feed and clothe him, make sure he went to school and had the right medical treatment to keep him healthy, but you could never make up for the fact that he didn't have anyone who loved him. Love was the biggest single ingredient a child needed to be happy, and that was why he was determined that his own daughter would always be surrounded by people who loved her.

He sighed. Even though he had made up his mind what he intended to do, it didn't mean it was going to be easy to achieve his objective. He still had to convince Lucy that he was sincere about his intentions. He could understand why she was so wary. Nothing he had done in the past had inspired confidence in her about his ability to make a long-term commitment. But somehow he had to make her understand that he only wanted what was best for their daughter.

That he wanted what was best for Lucy too was a very different matter, of course. He'd given up any rights to have a say in her life when he had left England. The best he could hope for now was that they might become friends one day.

The thought of them being friends made him feel very strange. Deep down, he knew that being Lucy's friend would never be enough.

The week came to an end at last and the weekend arrived. As it had been Lucy's first week back at work, Saturday was taken up with housework. She had been planning to take Izzy to the park but the weather was dreadful and, apart from a quick visit to the local shops, they didn't go out.

She got Izzy out of her cot on Sunday morning and gave her some cereal. Connor had told her on Friday afternoon that he would come round at two o'clock and she couldn't help feeling nervous at the thought of his impending visit. Had she been right to agree to let him see Izzy, or should she have refused? She couldn't decide—there were too many reasons for and against. All she could hope was that she wouldn't live to regret her decision.

In an effort to calm herself down, she got Izzy dressed and put her in her pram. Although the weather wasn't marvellous again that day, it seemed preferable to go out rather than sit there, worrying herself to death. They headed for the playground so Izzy could play on the swings. Their route took them alongside the river and Lucy could see that the banks had been breached in several places by the rising water level. Her flat was only a short distance from the river and she uttered a heartfelt prayer that the water wouldn't rise much further. She didn't need her home flooded to add to her woes!

She took Izzy home again and gave her some lunch then put her down for a nap. It was barely one o'clock when the doorbell rang and she groaned, knowing it had to be Connor. She still wasn't sure if she was doing the right thing, but now she would have to let him in.

'Izzy's having a nap,' she told him shortly as he stepped into the hall. 'I've only just put her down so I don't want to wake her just yet.'

'That's fine. I know I'm early, but I had to go into work to check on Alan Johnson. His temperature spiked again through the night and Bea wanted me to take a look at him,' he explained, following her into the sitting room. 'I couldn't see any point driving all the way home and then having to come back here so I apologise if I've inconvenienced you.'

'You haven't inconvenienced me. I would just prefer it if

you would stick to the time we've arranged in future so that we both know where we stand.'

'Of course. It won't happen again, I promise you.'

He sat down on the sofa and after a moment's hesitation Lucy sat down as well, wishing that she hadn't sounded so defensive. Did she have to make it quite so obvious how nervous she was?

'Look, Lucy, I don't want there to be a whole load of friction between us every time I come to see Izzy. It won't do her any good if she hears us arguing all the time.'

'I am not arguing. I'm just making it clear that I expect you to stick to a few basic rules.'

'Really? So that's why you jumped down my throat, is it? Because I'd broken one of your rules? In that case, maybe you should tell me what other rules you've dreamt up so I don't break them as well.' He laughed sceptically when she didn't reply. 'Why not be honest and admit that you don't want me here, do you?'

'No, I don't. And can you blame me?'

'Because I went off to America and left you? But I never lied to you, Lucy. I was completely honest about my intentions. You always knew that my career was important to me and that I wouldn't allow anything to stand in the way of achieving my goals.'

'Which is why I am so sceptical about these newly discovered paternal feelings you claim to have for Izzy,' she shot back.

'It's not a claim. It's the truth. I intend to be a proper father to her.' He stood up abruptly and went to the window, and she could see the tension in the long, elegant lines of his back. Part of her wanted to believe that he was telling her the truth, but the more cautious side needed proof.

'Why? That's what I don't understand, Connor.' She shrugged when he glanced round, trying to ignore the ache that filled her heart when she saw the hurt in his eyes. She couldn't afford to worry about his feelings when Izzy's happiness was at stake. 'You've never struck me as someone who needs other people in your life, and certainly not a child. You're completely self-sufficient.'

'Maybe that was true once, but people change. *I've* changed since I found out I had a daughter.'

He sat down again. Lucy could tell that he was hoping that would be the end of the matter but she needed to be sure that he had thought everything through properly.

'Having a child does change your life, and that's what worries me most of all. I'm not sure if you really understand what it takes to be a good father.'

'I'm not sure either, so that makes two of us.' He dredged up a smile but there was a wealth of sadness in his eyes. 'I never had much chance to find out, I'm afraid. My own father died when I was just a baby so I never knew him. My mother remarried when I was six and my stepfather certainly wasn't interested in being a father to me.'

'I had no idea,' she said softly, somewhat stunned by the admission. Connor had always refused to talk about his family whenever she had asked him about them in the past. At the time, she had seen it as a sign that he'd wanted to maintain his distance from her, but maybe there had been another reason. Had it been too painful for him to talk about them, perhaps? She sensed it was so, and the thought that she had misjudged him was very hard to accept.

'Why should you?' He shrugged. 'I never talk about my family, mainly because there's nothing to talk about. Suffice to say that my mother had me taken into care after she remarried and I haven't seen her or my stepfather since.' He gave a bitter little laugh. 'My credentials for being a good parent leave a lot to be desired, don't they?'

'But that's awful!' she exclaimed in dismay. 'How could your mother have done such a dreadful thing?'

'I have no idea and, to be brutally honest, I really don't care. She's not part of my life and she hasn't been for a very long time now. However, if my experiences taught me anything, it's that I don't want my child to grow up thinking that she isn't wanted. I care about Izzy. I care an awful lot, which is why I came back to England to see her.'

He leant forward in his seat and she could see the determination in his eyes. 'I didn't come back here to hurt you, Lucy. I know I was angry with you to begin with, but that's in the past. All I want now is to have the chance to be a proper father to Izzy. So will you let me do that? Please?'

Connor held his breath. He knew the situation could go either of two ways. Either Lucy would believe him and agree to let him share in Izzy's future, or she wouldn't.

Quite frankly, he didn't know what he was going to do if it was the latter. He could carry out his threat and apply for access through the courts, of course, but that would only alienate Lucy even more. He couldn't bear to think that she might end up hating him one day.

'It's not that I don't believe you're sincere about this, Connor. I just can't help worrying if you really understand what you're taking on.'

He blanked out that thought. He couldn't deal with it when he needed to focus all his energy on convincing her that he could be a good father to their daughter. 'I'm the first to admit that I know very little about raising a child, but I can learn. That's what all parents have to do, surely? They have to learn how to adapt.'

'But that's my whole point. Can you adapt? Can you put Izzy first and your career second?' She brushed back her hair and he could see the worry in her eyes. 'I know how driven you are, Connor. Your job is your life, and there's no room in it for anything else, is there?'

'Yes, I can adapt. I have the best reason in the world to do so.' He captured her hands and held them tightly, needing to convince her. 'I swear on my life that I will never do anything to hurt Izzy!'

'I know you mean that now, but what's going to happen a few years down the line?' She paused then hurried on because it needed to be said. 'What if you meet someone and she isn't interested in having Izzy around, for instance?'

'That will never happen,' he said firmly, because it was true. He couldn't imagine ever getting close to a woman again after what had happened with Lucy. He wouldn't want to. He would be constantly comparing her to Lucy and it would be cruel to do that when he knew in his heart that no one else could ever match up to her.

The thought sent a tremor scudding through him and he cleared his throat. 'It won't happen,' he repeated.

'I'm sorry, Connor, but you can't make promises like that.' She carefully withdrew her hands. 'You don't know what's going to happen in the future or how you are going to feel.'

'Neither can you.' He sat back in his seat, trying not to feel hurt by her withdrawal. There was no point comparing the way she behaved towards him now to how she had behaved in the past. He had accepted that they could never go back to the way things had been, so why did he feel so bereft?

'What do you mean by that?'

'That you can't say how you're going to feel in X amount of years either.' He laughed, clamping down on his emotions because he couldn't afford to weaken. 'Who's to say that you won't meet someone and decide that he is more important than Izzy? As I know to my cost, it can and does happen.'

'It will never happen to me! I love Izzy and I will be there for her for as long as she needs me!'

She shot to her feet, obviously upset that he should have compared her to his mother. Connor stood up as well, knowing that he should apologise yet unsure if it would be wise to do so. He'd already told her far more about himself than he would normally have done and he didn't want to compound his errors by making himself even more vulnerable.

'I didn't come here to argue with you, Lucy, so I suggest we agree to disagree.' He glanced at his watch. 'Is it time to wake Izzy up yet? You were the one who was so keen to stick to a timetable—remember?'

'I'll go and see.'

She spun round on her heel, making it clear that she hadn't forgiven him, and he sighed. He certainly didn't believe that she was like his mother. In fact, if he'd had to choose someone to have his child then he couldn't have chosen anyone better than Lucy.

His heart ground to a halt as that thought sank in. He'd been so angry when he'd found out that she had kept his child's existence a secret from him that he hadn't been able to think about anything else. Now, all of a sudden, he could see the situation clearly and he realised with a jolt that he was *glad* that Lucy was the mother of his child. Even though they hadn't planned on having a child together, it was the best thing that could have happened.

He looked round as she came back into the room with Izzy and a feeling of euphoria suddenly filled him. Ever since he'd been put into care, he'd been alone. Now he had a daughter to love and he would never be lonely again. His whole life had changed for ever. All the dreams he'd had for the future, all the goals he'd set for himself, no longer seemed important any more. What was important now was Izzy, and how *her* life turned out.

She would never feel lonely as he had done. She would never experience the pain of rejection that had haunted him. She would never have to prove her worth by succeeding at her career. She would always know that she was loved, wanted and cherished for herself. And if one day Lucy decided that she was glad he was Izzy's father then his happiness would be complete, although he had to be prepared for the fact that it might never happen.

He took a deep breath and used it to shore up the pain that rocked through him. He mustn't be greedy, mustn't wish for more than he had. Lucy had given him this precious child and he had to accept that it might be too much to hope that she could ever give him her trust.

CHAPTER SEVEN

'THIS little piggy went to market, this little piggy stayed at home…'

Lucy smiled when she saw Izzy start to wriggle in delight. The nursery rhyme was one of her daughter's favourites and she could see the little girl's excitement rising as Connor came to the last line.

'And this little piggy went wee-wee-wee all the way home!'

He tickled Izzy's bare feet, sending her into a paroxysm of laughter. Lucy quickly put out her hand and steadied her when she threatened to topple over.

'Careful, darling,' she said, placing another cushion behind her daughter's back.

They were sitting on the floor, surrounded by a heap of toys. They had played at least a dozen games of peekaboo then built a tower out of plastic blocks, which Izzy had promptly knocked down. Connor had been patience itself as he had played with her and despite herself Lucy had been impressed. However, a few hours spent playing games didn't prove that he would be a good father, did it?

'I think it's time this little lady had her tea.' She stood up and picked Izzy up off the floor, shaking her head when the little girl began to grizzle. It was time to bring Connor's visit to an end before she got too carried away. 'No, you can play again tomorrow, darling. It's time for your tea now.'

'Do you want me to clear up these toys while you feed her?' Connor offered, standing up as well.

'No, it's fine. I'll do them later when she's in bed.' Lucy quickly stepped aside. It had been fine while they had been devoting all their attention to Izzy, but all of a sudden she felt very aware of his maleness as he stood there, towering over her.

'In other words I'm dismissed?' He laughed when she didn't reply. 'It's OK, Lucy. I'm not going to outstay my welcome, if that's what worries you. I have to call at the shops and buy some groceries on my way home. I meant to go after I'd been to see Alan Johnson but I completely forgot.'

'Alan seemed much better on Friday so what's gone wrong now?' she asked quickly. There was no point letting the situation deteriorate into another argument when it would only upset Izzy. Far better to stick to a topic that wouldn't cause them any problems.

'I don't think there is anything actually wrong with him. You do get the odd fluctuation in temperature during the recovery period, but I just wanted to make absolutely certain there was nothing else brewing.'

'I understand. Alan's a great kid and he's been really brave, too. It's such a shame that he gets so few visitors. Nobody came to see him on Thursday or Friday.'

'I know.' His tone was grim as he led the way from the room. 'I got onto the manager of the care home but she was very offhand. She told me they were short-staffed and couldn't spare anyone to visit him.'

'That's really awful. You'd think that someone would have

made the effort to see Alan even if they had to do it in their free time.'

'It's the old story, I'm afraid—people will only do what they're paid for.'

'Is that partly why you called in to see him yourself?' she asked, recalling what he'd told her about his own childhood. Even now she found it hard to believe that his mother had abandoned him like that. She couldn't bear to imagine the kind of childhood he must have had, knowing that his own mother hadn't cared about him. It was no wonder that he was so determined to be part of Izzy's life, and her heart ached at the thought.

'I wanted to check how he was,' he said, firmly repudiating the suggestion.

'Of course,' she murmured, even though she didn't believe it had been his only reason. However, telling him that she understood why he'd wanted to see the boy could be a mistake when she needed to maintain a certain distance between them. It would be far too easy to find herself involved in his affairs.

It was a worrying thought and she quickly opened the front door. 'Thanks for playing with Izzy. I could tell how much she enjoyed it.'

'It was my pleasure, wasn't it, sweetheart?' He bent and kissed Izzy on the cheek then looked at Lucy. 'I know this hasn't been easy for you, and I really appreciate you letting me spend this time with her today. I'd like to do it again next weekend, if that's OK with you?'

'I don't think I have much choice, do I?' she said tartly, and he sighed.

'I know you aren't exactly thrilled about this situation, but the least we can do is to try and behave in a civilised manner.

It's going to put a huge strain on both of us if we're at loggerheads for the next eighteen years.'

'Always assuming your interest in Izzy lasts that long,' she shot back because she didn't appreciate having him lecture her.

He shook his head. 'I don't know how many more times I need to tell you this, but I'm in this for the long haul so get used to the idea, Lucy. You and Izzy are going to see a lot of me from now on.'

He turned and strode down the path before she could say anything and she sighed. He seemed so sure that his interest in Izzy would last that it made her wonder why she doubted him. Was she allowing her past experiences to colour her judgement too much, perhaps?

She knew it was true, and it was upsetting to think that she was being unfair to him. After all, Connor had never misled her about his intentions. She'd always known that he would leave her so what right did she have to use that fact against him now? Maybe she should give him the benefit of the doubt and accept that he meant what he said this time, too.

She stepped out of the door to call him back then swung round when she heard someone shouting. There was a man running up the path from the river and she could see that he was very agitated. Connor must have heard him shouting because he hurried over to him. Lucy watched as they had a brief conversation before the man raced back down the path.

'What's happened?' she demanded as Connor came hurrying across the road.

'There's a rowing boat adrift on the river with some kids in it. Can you phone the emergency services and tell them what's happened? I'm going to see what I can do to help.'

'Of course!'

Lucy ran back inside and dialled 999. Once she was sure that help was on its way, she strapped Izzy into her buggy and headed for the river. The boat had run aground on one of the small islands in the middle of the channel. Its bow appeared to be stuck in the mud but the stern was swinging wildly to and fro in the current. She could see several children in the boat and her heart sank when she realised the danger they were in.

'We need to get them out of there as quickly as possible,' Connor said grimly, coming over to her. 'They won't stand a chance if that boat is swept downriver.'

'The emergency services will be here soon,' she assured him.

'It will take at least ten minutes for them to get here and that could be too long. We need to get a line out to them so we can secure the boat and stop it being carried away.'

'There's a lifebelt station further down the river bank,' she told him, pointing in the right direction. 'Would that be any use?'

'It might be.'

He turned to the man who had raised the alarm and explained what they needed to do. The man immediately set off down the path to fetch the lifebelt. More people had arrived now and Connor nodded when someone asked him if the authorities had been contacted.

'They're on their way so can one of you go back up to the road and wait for them? We can't afford to waste any time once they get here.'

One of the women hurried up the path. The man had returned with the lifebelt and he handed it straight to Connor. Everyone seemed to take it for granted that he was in charge, although Lucy wasn't surprised. He was always so sure of himself that he inspired confidence in others.

Had it been his upbringing that had made him so self-assured? she found herself wondering. From what he had told her, he'd had nobody to turn to when he'd been growing up so he had learned to rely on himself. It had given him an inner strength which other people recognised. However, the downside was that he really didn't need anyone else. The only time that might change was if he fell in love, and it was upsetting to think that it might have happened already if those rumours about him and Dee were true.

'This is never going to work! Those kids are too scared to let go of the boat long enough to catch the lifebelt.'

Connor found it hard to contain his frustration. Despite all their efforts, they still hadn't managed to get a line to the children and the situation was becoming critical. The bow of the boat was gradually working loose from the mud and it wouldn't be long before it was swept away. He knew that he couldn't run the risk of that happening and came to a swift decision.

'I'm going to swim out to the boat and tie it on to one of those trees,' he announced, turning to the group that had gathered on the riverbank. 'With a bit of luck I should be able to get the children onto the island and keep them there until help arrives, but I'm going to need some volunteers to help me.'

Several of the men immediately stepped forward. Connor gathered them together and explained what he wanted them to do. 'You'll need to form a chain with each man holding onto the man in front of him. The first man in the chain will have to tie the end of the rope around his waist and act as the anchor.'

Once he was sure everyone understand what they were doing, he took off his shoes and stripped off his sweatshirt, shivering as a blast of rain hit his bare chest. It looked as though they were in for another downpour, he thought grimly, then glanced round when Lucy appeared at his side.

'Shouldn't you wait until the emergency services get here?'

'I don't think we can afford to wait,' he told her, trying to ignore the feeling of warmth that flowed through him when he saw the worry in her eyes. 'If that boat comes adrift, those kids will be swept away, and I don't rate their chances very highly, do you?'

'No…'

She gave a little shudder, although whether it stemmed from fear for the children's safety or for his he had no idea and didn't dwell on it. He needed to keep a clear head at that moment and not allow his thoughts to get cluttered up by any other issues.

He left her standing on the bank and made his way to the edge of the water. One of the men helped him into the lifebelt then they all took up their positions. Connor could feel the current tugging at his legs as soon as he entered the water. He only managed a couple of steps before he was swept off his feet but he was prepared for that and didn't try to fight it.

He struck out towards the centre of the river, letting the current carry him towards the boat. He was a strong swimmer but even with the lifebelt for added buoyancy, he had difficulty making any headway and only just managed to grab hold of the stern before the current swept him away. There were four children in the boat and they were terrified. He had to shout to make himself heard above the sound of their screams.

'Sit down! Nobody is to stand up in case you tip the boat over. I'm going to tie it to those trees then we'll get you onto the island.'

Clinging onto the side of the boat, he managed to drag himself to the bow and scrambled through the mud onto the island. He then had to unfasten the rope from the lifebelt and tie it to a cleat. He had just finished securing the boat to a tree when it floated free of the mud and he heard the children scream in terror as it began to swing wildly around in the current.

'Sit down!' he yelled when he saw one little girl standing up. The boat lurched again as the current twisted it around and the next second she tumbled over the side into the water.

Connor didn't hesitate as he jumped back into the river and swam towards her. The current had carried her several yards away from the boat and he had to call on his last reserves of strength to reach her before she was sucked under the water. He managed to grab hold of her arm and hauled her back to the surface, but he didn't have the strength to swim back to the island. Water swirled into his face as he struggled to keep them both afloat and he coughed as he swallowed a mouthful. There was a sudden roaring sound close by and the next moment a dinghy appeared alongside him.

Connor grabbed hold of the lifebelt that one of the crew tossed to him and hung on while they were towed to the bank where willing hands helped them out of the water. He lay on the grass for a moment, sucking in great breaths of air, then forced himself to his feet. Lucy was kneeling beside the girl and he hurried over to her.

'How is she?'

'She's not breathing and I can't find a pulse.'

'We need to resuscitate her. Can you do the breathing while I do the compressions?'

Connor knelt down as Lucy positioned herself by the

child's head. He waited while she checked the girl's airway for any obstructions then performed four sharp inflations and checked her pulse again. She shook her head. 'Still no pulse.'

'Right.'

He placed his right hand on the child's chest and pressed down gently five times. As soon as he stopped, Lucy performed another single inflation. The technique for resuscitating a child was slightly different to that used for an adult—the ventilations and compressions needed to be done slightly faster and with less pressure—but both he and Lucy had performed the technique many times before and they soon found the right rhythm. When the girl suddenly started coughing, he grinned at her.

'That's what I call a result. We make a great team, don't we, Lucy?'

'So it appears.' Lucy did her best not to let him see how that comment had made her feel, but it had touched a very raw nerve.

She looked up in relief when one of the rescue crew came to tell them that the ambulances had arrived. The paramedics appeared a few minutes later and she helped them load the child onto a stretcher. One of the paramedics popped an oxygen mask over the girl's face then wrapped her in a thermal blanket to help ward off hypothermia. The river water was very cold even in the height of summer and the child's core body temperature would have fallen dramatically during her immersion. Lucy frowned as she glanced over at Connor, who was giving a statement to the police, because his body temperature would have dropped as well.

'Can you let me have one of those blankets?' she asked the paramedic. The rest of the children had been brought ashore now and the crew of the second ambulance were dealing with them. Her part in the proceedings seemed to be over so, after thanking one of the bystanders for watching Izzy for her, she made her way over to Connor.

'You'd better put this round you,' she said, handing him the blanket.

'Thanks.' He draped it round his shoulders and shuddered. 'You're going to the top of my Christmas card list for thinking of this.'

Lucy looked away when he smiled at her. It would be stupid to imagine that it meant anything. Connor had had his chance to make her a permanent part of his life and he hadn't taken it. She doubted if he was about to change his mind— not that she wanted him to, of course!

Her face filled with colour and she turned to hurry up the path. Connor followed her, pausing several times while people congratulated him. Each time he shrugged off their praise but she knew they were right to commend him. He had risked his life to save those children and he deserved every credit for his bravery.

She stopped when they reached the road, knowing that she should say something, too. 'You were very brave to do what you did.'

'I think it was more a case of instinct taking over.'

'There was more to it than that,' she said firmly. 'You risked your life for those children, and that takes real courage.'

'I wouldn't go that far but thanks anyway. I appreciate it, especially as we aren't exactly on the best of terms.'

'Maybe I have been a little hard on you,' she conceded. 'It's just that I can't help worrying about Izzy.'

'I know. And I understand how you feel, Lucy, really I do.'

He touched her lightly on the cheek and she shivered when she felt the coldness of his fingers against her skin. She stepped back, anxious not to prolong the contact. While she was willing to admit that she might have been a little unreasonable, that was as far as she was prepared to go. She certainly wouldn't risk falling under his spell again.

'You need to get out of those wet clothes,' she said, hurriedly changing the subject. There was no danger of her falling under Connor's spell a second time, she assured herself. She had learned her lesson the hard way and even though she still loved him, she wasn't stupid enough to risk having her heart broken again.

'I also need to wash away the smell of that mud. It absolutely stinks!'

Lucy summoned a smile as he sniffed his arm in disgust. The only way to deal with this situation was by trying to behave as naturally as possible around him. 'Stop complaining. Some people pay a fortune for mud baths and you just had one for free.'

'Well, I certainly wouldn't pay good money to end up smelling like something that has been festering at the bottom of a gym bag!'

'Do you want to come back to the flat and have a shower?' she suggested because it was what she would have done for anyone in the circumstances.

'Thanks. It's really tempting but I need to check how our patient is doing. Although she appears to have recovered pretty well, she isn't out of the woods yet. If water has passed from her lungs into her blood, it could cause a problem. Plus the lining of her lungs might have been damaged so I'd like to run some tests.'

'You mean that you're going back to work?' she exclaimed. 'Is that really necessary? Martin's on duty this weekend and he's more than capable of arranging for any tests to be done without you being there.'

'I'm sure Martin is perfectly capable,' he said shortly. 'However, he might not have any experience of dealing with this type of situation. I'd just feel happier if I sorted it out myself.'

'I understand,' she said, knowing there was no point trying to dissuade him once he had made up his mind. However, the fact that he was prepared to go into work after what had happened only seemed to prove how foolish it would be to hope that anything would ever come before his job—*including* Izzy.

Lucy was surprised by how much that thought upset her. Having her biggest fear confirmed like this should have eased her conscience, yet she couldn't help feeling sad that Connor was reverting to form. As she followed him across the road, she found herself thinking how empty his life was going to be if he continued to drive himself so hard. Surely he could see that he needed more than his job to make him happy?

He stopped beside his car and turned to her. 'Thanks again for everything, Lucy. Despite the way it's ended, this has been one of the best days of my entire life.'

Lucy could hear the emotion in his voice and, in spite of her concerns, she couldn't help being moved by it. 'Izzy enjoyed it, too.'

'Did she?'

'Yes. I could tell that she did.' She took a quick breath but there was no way that she could lie to him. 'It isn't usual for her to take to anyone as quickly as she took to you.'

'Maybe she realised there was a special bond between us,' he said huskily.

Lucy shrugged, neither confirming nor denying the suggestion. Maybe there was a bond between him and Izzy but it wouldn't survive unless he was prepared to make a real commitment to her. And at the moment everything pointed towards the fact that he was never going to be able to do that.

Connor got into the car and rolled down the window. 'I'll see you at work tomorrow, will I?'

'Yes. I'm due in at eight.'

'Right. I'll see you then.'

He gave her a quick smile then drove away. Lucy took Izzy home. The little girl was dozing so she left her in the buggy while she made her tea. In some respects the day had gone better than she'd feared it would. Connor genuinely seemed to care about Izzy but she wasn't convinced that he would put his daughter's interests first if it came to a choice between her and his job.

It might not matter so much while Izzy was a baby but what about when she grew up? How would she feel if her father constantly let her down because he put his job first? If Connor wanted to be a proper father to Izzy then he had to be prepared to put her first every single time and not just when it suited him.

Lucy squared her shoulders. *She* might have accepted that she'd come second to his job while they had been together, but she would never accept that position for their daughter!

CHAPTER EIGHT

'DID the parents say how long she might have been like this? It would help if we had some kind of a timescale to work to.'

It was Monday morning and the day had got off to a flying start. No sooner had Connor arrived at work than he'd been called down to A and E to see a twelve-year-old girl called Amy Marshall who had been found unconscious in her bedroom. The paramedics who had attended the call had discovered a can of deodorant lying on the bed beside her so it looked as though she might have been inhaling the gas from it.

'The parents aren't here,' the young A and E registrar explained. 'It was the *au pair* who phoned for an ambulance and she came in with her.'

'So does she have any idea how long the child has been unconscious?' Connor demanded, rolling back the girl's eyelids so he could check her response to light.

'We don't know.' The younger doctor shrugged when Connor looked at him. 'She doesn't speak much English so we haven't been able to get any information out of her apart from the kid's name and age.'

'Yet the parents saw fit to leave her in charge of their daughter?'

Connor found it difficult to hide his annoyance as he shone the light into Amy's eyes. He couldn't believe the cavalier attitude some parents displayed even after all the years he'd been working in paediatrics. 'Both pupils are responding evenly to light so that's something to be grateful for,' he said, tilting her chin so that he could shine the light up her nose and examine her nasal passages. 'No sign of erosion of the nasal membranes so it doesn't look as though it's chronic inhalant abuse we're dealing with.' He opened her mouth and checked her throat. 'Nothing there either, although you don't need to be addicted to do yourself a great deal of harm. One whiff of that gas is all it takes sometimes to stop the heart.'

'You wonder why these kids do it,' the young registrar said sadly. 'Especially a kid like this who has everything she could possibly want. The address the paramedics gave us is in one of the best parts of the town. You have to be seriously rich to live there.'

'Sometimes it's peer pressure and other times it's just the thrill of doing something they know is wrong. Money really doesn't come into it.'

He checked Amy's reflexes and was pleased when he got a slightly better response than he'd feared. Inhaling the propellants found in common household aerosols like deodorants and hairsprays could cause severe damage to the central nervous system amongst other things.

He made a note on her chart then checked her sats, which had improved since she'd been admitted. Inhalant abuse created an effect similar to that of anaesthetics, which acted by slowing down the body's functions. If enough gas was inhaled directly into the lungs then death by suffocation could occur. The toxic effects of the gas could also induce heart failure, so Amy had been extremely lucky this time. However, Connor knew enough about the long-term dangers not to become complacent. Repeated inhalant abuse caused kidney and liver damage, so she would need to be admitted while tests were done.

'I'm going to admit her to Paeds,' he told the younger doctor. 'Is the *au pair* still here? I'd really like to get a patient history from her.'

'She's waiting outside although I doubt if she'll be able to tell you very much.' The younger man shrugged. 'Her English seems to be limited to "yes" and "no" with the odd "please" thrown in for good measure.'

Connor sighed. 'I don't suppose you know what nationality she is?'

'One of the nurses thought she was Polish.'

'So do we have any Polish-speaking staff working here?'

'I've no idea,' the younger man replied cheerfully. 'I rarely get out of A and E so I haven't a clue about the rest of the staff.'

Connor thanked him anyway and went to find the *au pair*. She was extremely upset and almost incoherent because of it. He explained as clearly as he could that Amy would be taken to the paediatric unit, although he wasn't sure if the poor woman understood what he was saying. As he went back upstairs, he tried to work out how they could solve the problem of communicating with her. The girl's parents needed to be informed about what had happened and they had no way of getting in contact with them unless they could make the *au pair* understand what they wanted her to do.

Lucy was helping Sandra prepare a bed for the girl when he arrived so he drew her aside, thinking about what had happened the day before. It had been wonderful to spend all that time with Izzy, but the best thing of all was that it felt as though he'd made a breakthrough with Lucy as well. She had seemed far more approachable after they had worked together by the river, saving that child's life, and he couldn't help hoping that it might mark an improvement in their relationship.

'We have a problem with the patient who's coming up from A and E,' he explained, confining his thoughts to work. It wasn't like him to let personal issues interfere with his job but he seemed to be finding it increasingly difficult of late to separate the two. He sighed. At one time he hadn't even had a private life let alone had to worry about it, and it just proved once again how much his life had changed.

'What sort of problem?'

'It looks like a classic case of inhalant abuse but I really need a patient history, and the *au pair,* who came in with the girl, doesn't speak much English.'

'What about her parents?' Lucy asked, frowning. 'Surely they're the ones to ask?'

'They would be if I knew how to get in touch with them.' He shrugged. 'Nobody knows where they are—that's what I need to ask the *au pair.* One of the nurses thinks she might be Polish—do we have any Polish-speaking staff working at the hospital?'

'I'm not sure. There's been a lot of changes in past few months and I've lost track. Maybe Sandra will know.' She beckoned Sandra over. 'Do you know of any staff who speak Polish? We need someone to translate for us.'

'Dee, of course. Her mum is Polish and she learned it from her,' Sandra informed them, giving Connor a funny look as though he should have known that fact himself.

'Thanks. I'll give Dee a call and see if she can help us out.' Connor forbore to say anything in his defence. It was far too complicated to explain that he knew nothing about Dee's background. He turned to Lucy and immediately wished that he had taken the opportunity to clear things up when he saw the hurt in her eyes. She obviously believed those stupid rumours about him and Dee, and he hated to think that they were creating a problem between them. However, with Sandra standing there, there was very little he could do.

'Can you get Amy settled in? I'm going to run some tests to see what damage she's done to herself as soon as I've spoken to her parents and got their permission.'

'Of course.'

She gave him a cool smile then went back to finish preparing the bed. Connor groaned to himself. The longer he let the situation continue, the more problems it was going to cause and it was so frustrating. Surely Lucy must know that he wasn't interested in another woman?

His heart contracted in sudden panic but there was no point lying to himself. Lucy was the only woman he had ever wanted to spend his life with. It was the reason why he had gone off to Boston, and it was the reason why he knew there would never be anyone to replace her. It was ironic that he would never be able to tell her that.

She might have been hurt by those rumours, but he mustn't make the mistake of thinking that she still cared about him. It was only natural that she should feel resentful. He had left her when she'd been having his child and it made no difference that he'd been ignorant of the fact at the time. It didn't excuse what he'd done but it did explain why she hadn't wanted to tell him about Izzy. Why should she have told him when he had made it plain that he'd wanted nothing more to do with her?

All of a sudden, he could see the situation from her side

and he went cold when he realised what an uphill struggle it was going to be to gain her trust. He'd kept banging on about the fact that he had never misled her but that wasn't the point. He had abandoned her at the worst possible time, and he couldn't blame her if she wanted nothing more to do with him.

'She says that Amy's parents left her a mobile phone number but the phone was switched off when she tried to call them.'

Lucy nodded as Dee finished translating what the *au pair* had said. They had discovered very little about Amy Marshall so far, apart from the fact that she suffered from asthma. The *au pair*, Lydia Godycka, hadn't been able to tell them the name or the address of the family's GP because she had only been working for them for a week. However, it was a help to know that Amy was asthmatic and Lucy knew that Connor would be pleased to have that information. Dee would probably earn herself some extra brownie points for finding it out.

'Does Lydia know where the parents work?' she said, hurriedly squashing that unworthy thought. It had been kind of Dee to come into the hospital and she didn't deserve to be accused of having ulterior motives when she was trying to help them.

'I'll ask her.' Dee turned to the young woman again and Lucy waited while they had a brief conversation.

'Lydia says that the parents own a factory that makes electrical equipment,' Dee explained at last. She paused when Lydia said something else, and sighed. 'I don't think they spend very much time at home from what Lydia has just told me.'

'Does she know the name or the address of the factory?' Lucy asked. 'Maybe we could send someone round there to speak to them, or find another phone number so we can contact them.'

'I'll see.' Once again there was a brief pause while the two women conferred. 'She doesn't know the address, but she thinks the factory is called C&J Technology—does that help you?'

'Yes. I'll check with directory enquiries and see if they can find a phone number.' Lucy smiled at the *au pair*. 'Can you thank Lydia for me? She's been a great help.'

Dee thanked the woman then stood up. 'I'll have to go now,' she told Lucy as they left the relatives' room together. 'I've got an appointment at the hairdresser's and I don't want to be late.'

'Are you going somewhere special tonight?' Lucy asked, trying her best to be friendly towards the other woman.

'I don't know yet. It's a surprise. He wouldn't tell me where we're going so I could end up in a burger bar, and then my very expensive hair-do will have been a complete waste of money!'

Lucy summoned a smile when Dee laughed. However, the thought of Dee and Connor spending the evening together was very hard to swallow. 'So long as you enjoy each other's company, that's all that matters, isn't it?'

'Oh, I love being with him—there's no doubt about that,' Dee said wistfully.

'But?' Lucy prompted, knowing in her heart that she shouldn't be asking questions like that. Connor's relationship with Dee had nothing to do with her yet she wouldn't have been human if she hadn't been interested.

'But there's a lot of things we need to sort out before we ride off into the sunset—*if* we ever get that far, of course. There's no guarantee that it's ever going to happen now.'

She didn't say anything else so Lucy had no idea what she'd meant. She went into the office after Dee left, thinking about what she had just learned. Dee had seemed to imply that she and Connor were considering making a permanent commitment to each other so did that mean they were thinking of getting married?

Lucy's heart spasmed with pain even though she knew that she didn't have any right to feel this way. Connor hadn't made *her* any promises, so he was free to do whatever he wanted to. If he chose to marry Dee then that was his business yet the thought brought a lump to her throat.

Once upon a time she had dreamed that he would want to marry her but she'd been fooling herself. He had never cared enough about her to marry her otherwise he wouldn't have gone to Boston. She had been just someone he had met along the way, a stopgap until he'd found the woman he wanted to spend his life with. Maybe he and Dee did have issues that they needed to resolve, but Connor must have been confident that they could work through them if he had asked her to come back to England with him.

Her heart sank because the biggest issue she could think of had to be Izzy. A lot of women wouldn't be happy at the thought of their partner having a child from a previous relationship, and Dee might be finding it hard to accept. There had been nothing in Dee's manner to suggest that she knew Lucy was Izzy's mother, so maybe Connor hadn't told her that yet. That could be the reason why he had arranged to take her out that night—so he could tell her all the facts.

Quite frankly, Lucy didn't know how she felt about the idea, but the last thing she wanted was Dee telling everyone else. She couldn't bear to think that everyone would be gossiping about her so she would have to make it clear to Connor that he must swear Dee to secrecy. Maybe people would have to know in time but not just yet. She wanted to protect her privacy a while longer, although it might be even worse if the information became common knowledge in the future. She could just imagine the furore it would cause if Connor and Dee were married when the news broke!

She sighed wearily. Whichever way she looked at it, this situation was going to cause a great deal of heartache for everyone concerned.

Lucy managed to get the phone number of the factory from directory enquiries and telephoned Amy's parents. The receptionist put her through to Mrs Marshall's office after she explained why she was calling. She knew what a shock it would be for the woman so she tried to break the news to her as gently as possible, but Mrs Marshall's reaction wasn't what she had expected. As she put down the phone after a decidedly frosty conversation, Lucy found it hard to hide her dismay.

'What's wrong? Has something happened to Izzy?'

She looked up when she realised that Connor must have come into the office while she'd been on the phone. 'No, Izzy's fine. That was Amy Marshall's mother on the phone— I managed to get the phone number of where she works from directory enquiries.'

'Oh, I see. For a horrible moment I thought Izzy might have had an accident in the crèche.'

'Izzy's fine,' she repeated, so there would be no mistake. There could be no mistake about the fact that Connor was concerned either, but would his interest in Izzy last if Dee was opposed to him seeing her? Dee might come to resent the time he spent with Izzy and try to stop him visiting her, and if that happened, it could have a disastrous effect on the little girl. The thought that Izzy might become the innocent victim in any future dispute made her feel more anxious than ever, although she had no intention of sharing her concerns with Connor. There was no way that she was going to give him the opportunity to accuse her of being jealous!

'That's a relief. So what did the mother have to say?' He frowned as he came over and sat on the edge of the desk. 'Did Mrs Marshall know that her daughter has been abusing inhalants?'

'I've no idea. I explained that Amy was in hospital and that it looked as though she had been inhaling gas from an aerosol but that was as far as I got. Mrs Marshall just cut me off and asked if Amy was all right. When I said that Amy was stable, she told me in that case she was too busy to deal with me and that's why she employed a nanny. I never even got a chance to ask her for the name of her GP before she hung up.'

'Really?' Connor's frown deepened. 'It's just not good enough. She can't abdicate her responsibilities like that, no matter how busy she might be. Do you have that phone number? I'd like to speak to her myself.'

'Here it is.'

Lucy gave him the number and waited while he made the call. This time the receptionist refused to put him through to Mrs Marshall's office, claiming that her employer couldn't be disturbed. Connor asked to speak to Mr Marshall instead but got the same response: Mr Marshall couldn't be disturbed either. He was furious when he hung up and Lucy sympathised with him.

'So what do we do now?' she asked.

'Have a word with Social Services and see what they have to say. It's an appalling situation and there is no excuse for it.'

'But can Social Services do anything?' She sighed when

he looked sharply at her. 'I know how you feel, Connor, but the parents haven't done anything wrong. They've employed someone to take care of Amy so technically she hasn't been neglected. And even if they had been at home this morning, they might not have been able to prevent this happening.'

'Maybe they do employ someone to look after the child but she is still their responsibility.'

'Yes, she is. But to all intents and purposes they are doing everything they are supposed to do. There is no question of neglect when the *au pair* is there to look after Amy.'

'It takes more than paying for a stranger's services to look after a child properly!' he said in a voice like thunder as he got up and went to the window.

Lucy could tell how angry he was and it surprised her to see him show so much emotion. He'd always been so controlled in the past, had always dealt with each case with the same professional detachment, no matter how heart-rending it had been. So what had changed? Had it been finding out that he had a child of his own which had unlocked his emotions? Had Izzy taught him how to love?

The thought filled her with joy all of a sudden. If she could be sure that Connor was capable of such depth of feeling then she would have less reason to worry about him hurting Izzy. He would want only what was best for their daughter. And maybe at some point in the future he would want what was best for her, too…

'Sorry to interrupt but I have a bit of a problem.'

Lucy looked round when a familiar voice suddenly cut into her thoughts. Dee was standing in the doorway and seeing her there brought Lucy back to earth with a thump. She was trembling as she got up from the desk but it was understandable. Plummeting from the heights of euphoria into the depths of despair was bound to have had an effect. Maybe Connor did know how to love now, and maybe finding out about Izzy had been the key that had unlocked his emotions. However, it wouldn't be *she* who reaped the benefits, but Dee. Dee was the woman he was planning on spending his life with, the woman he loved. Not Lucy.

CHAPTER NINE

'THERE was no sign of any water when I parked there. Mum will have a fit. She's had that car for years and never had an accident, yet the first time I drive it, this has to happen!'

'It wasn't your fault, Dee. You weren't to know that the car park would be flooded.'

Connor did his best to respond with his usual calm efficiency but it wasn't easy. He glanced at Lucy, wishing he knew what was going on. She looked so pale as she stood there by the desk that he was afraid she was going to keel over.

'I'll have to go and phone Mum.' Dee grimaced. 'Sorry to be a nuisance but I was just so surprised…'

'You can use the phone in here,' Lucy said suddenly, breaking her silence. As Connor watched, she summoned a smile but he could see the effort it cost her. 'Maybe your mother has breakdown cover so you might be able to get them to tow the car out.'

'Why didn't I think of that?' Dee exclaimed, hurrying to the desk.

'Because you'd had a shock.' Lucy managed another smile but it was even more strained than the first one had been. When she headed towards the door, Connor followed her. He needed to find out if she was all right.

'Lucy, wait!' he said urgently as she hurried towards the ward.

'I'm sorry, Connor, but I can't afford to waste any more time.' She barely paused as she glanced back but he could see how pale she looked even now. 'I need to make sure everything is ready for your ward round.'

'To hell with the ward round!' He put out his hand when she went to open the ward door. 'Are you feeling all right? You look really pale.'

'I'm fine. I just want to get on and sort things out, so if you'll excuse me…?' She looked pointedly at his hand, but he shook his head.

'You're not going anywhere until I'm sure that you're OK. If you feel ill, Lucy, then for heaven's sake say so. You don't win extra brownie points for being brave!'

If anything, she went even paler at that, although for the life of him he couldn't think what he'd said to cause such a reaction. Tilting back her head, she looked him straight in the eyes and he was shocked to see the chill in her gaze. In the whole of the time he had known her, he couldn't remember her ever looking at him that way before.

'I am not ill. I am merely trying to do my job.'

'In that case, I apologise for holding you up,' he said, stepping back to let her pass.

He made his way back to the office, trying to come to terms with the fact that she had looked at him with such a complete lack of emotion. He would be the first to admit that their relationship hadn't been easy since he'd come back to England. However, even when they had been arguing Lucy hadn't looked at him that way, as though she didn't care.

Maybe it was stupid to let it get to him but he couldn't help feeling bitterly hurt. It was obvious that she felt nothing for him now, not even anger, and the pain inside him seemed to grow until it reached gigantic proportions. He would far rather she hated him than viewed him with indifference!

Lucy had no idea how she got through the rest of the day. She couldn't seem to stop thinking about what had happened. Connor had never loved her because he hadn't been capable of feeling that kind of emotion when they had been together. However, now that Izzy had come into his life, everything had changed, and it was the bitterest of blows to know that some other woman would reap the benefits.

She did the handover in record time and bade Bea a swift goodbye at the end of her shift. The queue outside the crèche was fairly short for once so it didn't take her very long to collect Izzy. She headed for the exit, stopping when she opened the door and discovered that the forecourt was ankle deep in water. This part of the hospital was closest to the river and provided a natural run-off for the rising water. A pump truck had been sent from the local fire station to deal with the problem, but more water was pouring into the grounds as fast as they were pumping it out. There was no way that she could avoid getting wet if she wanted to get to her car so she gritted her teeth and stepped down onto the path. After everything else that had gone on that day, wet feet were the least of her problems!

She was halfway across the forecourt when her foot skidded on a pebble hidden beneath the water and she cried out in alarm when she felt herself pitching sideways.

'Careful!' All of a sudden Connor was there, his hand closing firmly around her arm as he steadied her. He set her back on her feet then lifted Izzy out of her arms. 'Let me carry her.

It's difficult enough to wade through all this water without having to carry a baby as well.'

'Thank you.' Lucy didn't argue even though the last thing she wanted was to have to speak to him again. However, it seemed safer to let him help rather than risk slipping a second time. They reached the car park and she was relieved to see that her car was in a section that hadn't been flooded. A lot of the other vehicles that had been parked there hadn't fared nearly so well—one whole row was axle-deep in water.

'It's a bit of a mess, isn't it?' Connor said, stopping by her car while she unlocked the doors.

'It is.' She tossed her bag onto the passenger seat then turned to take Izzy off him.

'Bye-bye, poppet,' he said, brushing the little girl's cheek with a gentle kiss.

Lucy felt foolish tears spring to her eyes as she took Izzy from him. He would never kiss her like that, she thought miserably as she bent down to strap Izzy into her seat. He would never use such tender endearments when he was speaking to her either. Connor might love their daughter but he didn't love her. He had given his heart to another woman and it was Dee who would be on the receiving end of all that tenderness now, Dee who would fill his nights with passion and his life with love. The thought was almost too much to bear.

'What's wrong, Lucy? And before you tell me that everything is fine, I have to tell you that I don't believe it. Something has upset you and I want to know what it is.'

His voice was so gentle, so caring, that she simply couldn't cope. She would end up pouring it all out if she wasn't careful and it was the last thing she wanted to do. She might not have his love but she did have her pride, and she would never beg him to love her. What would be the point? You couldn't make someone love you—they either did or they didn't. And no amount of pleas or recriminations would change how they felt. The sooner she accepted that Connor didn't love her, the easier it would be for all of them, but most important of all, for Izzy.

'Nothing has upset me.' She closed the rear door then forced herself to look at him. 'I'm just tired, Connor. It isn't easy holding down a demanding job as well as looking after a baby.'

'Of course it isn't. I should have thought of that before.' A look of chagrin crossed his face. 'You need a break, Lucy. What if I look after Izzy tonight so you can have some time to yourself? I could come round to your flat and babysit while you go out—'

'No!' She hastily moderated her tone when she saw him start. 'It's kind of you but there's no need—really, there isn't. I'll be fine once I've got home and had a cup of tea.'

'But it's only fair that I should do my share. It's not right that you should have to bear the brunt of the childcare all by yourself.'

'It isn't a problem,' she repeated. The last thing she wanted was to upset the plans he'd made for the evening.

Her heart lurched at the thought of what those plans might entail. She didn't want to think about him and Dee enjoying a romantic evening together, although it might not be *that* romantic if he was planning on telling Dee tonight that she was his baby's mother. The thought immediately reminded her that she had meant to ask him to swear Dee to secrecy. Even though the last thing she felt like doing was promoting another argument, it was too important to put it off.

'Look, Connor, I don't know what you've told Dee about Izzy but I don't want her telling everyone that you are Izzy's father—is that clear?'

'I haven't told Dee anything.' His mouth compressed. 'Despite what the rumour-mongers might be saying, Dee and I are *not* having a relationship.'

'Whatever.' Lucy shrugged. If he wanted to insist that he and Dee weren't an item, that was his business. However, she didn't intend to become a casualty of their affair.

'It's the truth, Lucy. Why won't you believe me?' he said in exasperation.

'If you say it's true then it must be,' she said with such a lack of conviction that he swore under his breath.

'It's like beating my head against a brick wall! You've made up your mind and that's it. Well, if it makes you happy to think that I'm seeing Dee then carry on. I'm not going to tell you again. There's no point.'

He turned and walked away, and she saw him get into his car. He backed out of the space and drove away without another glance in her direction. Lucy sighed wearily. It would be so much simpler if he would just admit that he was seeing Dee. She really couldn't understand why he was denying that they were having an affair…

Unless he was afraid to admit the truth in case it upset her and caused repercussions?

Her heart sank as she got into her car. Was Connor loath to admit that he was involved with another woman because he was worried about how *she* might react? Maybe he thought she would be so jealous that she would take out her spite on him by banning him from seeing Izzy? It was a horrible feeling to know that he believed she was capable of that and her mouth tightened as she started the engine. If she did deny him access then it would be out of concern for their daughter, not out of pique!

* * *

'Right, Alan, it looks as though you'll be leaving us very shortly. Your temperature has settled down again so, as long as nothing else happens, I should be able to discharge you on Monday.'

Connor smiled at Alan as he handed the boy's file to Martin Fellows. It was Friday morning and they were almost at the end of the daily ward round. So far he had seen and discharged four of the children, including the girl they had rescued from the river and Ben Roberts, the boy who'd had his appendix removed. The infection Ben had contracted had responded well to the increased antibiotic regime and he was well enough to go home, a piece of news which Ben had greeted with delight. Alan's reaction, however, was far less enthusiastic.

'I still feel funny,' Alan muttered. 'My head hurts and my eyes feel all funny, too. You won't send me back to that place if I'm not well, will you?'

'Of course not,' Connor said gently. He took the file from Martin again and rechecked the boy's obs, but everything was fine—temperature normal, BP spot on and no sign of a rash which could indicate the onset of septicaemia. Alan had made an excellent recovery and he was pleased with his progress, but he guessed that the boy's reluctance to be discharged stemmed from his desire not to be sent back to the care home. Sadly, there was very little he could do about that.

'We'll keep an eye on you over the weekend. If you don't feel well then make sure you tell one of the nurses. I'm going to ask Staff Nurse Adams to move you into the ward today so at least you'll have some company there.'

Alan still looked unhappy when they left the high-dependency unit and Connor paused outside the door so he could have a word with Lucy about him. The rest of the team had ambled off towards the ward kitchen where a pot of coffee would be waiting for them. It was the ideal opportunity to get Lucy on her own, although he could tell from her manner that she wasn't interested in anything other than work-related matters.

He did his best to hide his irritation. She had been very distant with him all week and he found it hard to believe that it was those stupid rumours that had upset her. Maybe he had done something else to offend her, although he couldn't for the life of him think what it was. Not that it would take very much, of course. Just breathing the same air as her might have been enough!

'Can you keep an eye on Alan for me?' he said as calmly as he could, bearing in mind the aggravation he was suffering. 'He's done extremely well so far and I don't want him having a relapse because he's worried about being sent back to that care home.'

'Of course. Is that all, Dr Mackenzie?'

No, it isn't all, he was tempted to say. *I want to know why you're treating me like a criminal instead of the father of your daughter!* However, coming out with a statement like that would do little to improve matters.

'Yes, thank you. Alan can be moved into the ward as soon as you can arrange it.'

'I'll get everything ready,' she assured him politely. She was just about to move away when Connor remembered that he hadn't finalised the arrangements for that weekend. It seemed easier to get it done than wait until later. At least she was speaking to him at the moment, albeit in a rather chilly way, but there was no knowing what might happen in a couple of hours' time.

'Before you go, Lucy, is it all right if I come round to see Izzy again on Sunday?' He shrugged when she looked at him, trying not to let that thought get him down. 'Would the same time suit you? I could make it later if it would be easier for you.'

'I'm afraid it isn't convenient this weekend. I'm going out.'

'Out? But you knew I'd want to see her again on Sunday. Surely you can change your arrangements?'

'I'm afraid not. It's Mark Dawson's leaving do and he's having a barbecue. I accepted the invitation some time ago— long before you came back onto the scene. I have no intention of backing out at this stage.'

The expression on her face challenged him to object but Connor wasn't about to make that mistake. He nodded, trying not to let her see how much it hurt to have her behave this way towards him. If he hadn't been so determined to play an active part in Izzy's life, he might have given up. But it was far too important to him that he should be a proper father to Izzy to let Lucy's attitude deter him.

'I wouldn't expect you to. I just hope the weather improves. There's nothing worse than a barbecue in the rain, is there?'

He gave her a cool smile then went into the kitchen, nodding his thanks when Amanda poured him a cup of coffee. He even accepted a biscuit when Tom offered it to him, not wanting to appear too stuffy to join in. Coffee and biscuits were one of the perks the junior medical staff enjoyed after a ward round, although he usually went straight back to his office and left them to it. However, that day he felt like making a point: he wasn't some overbearing boss who treated his staff like second-class citizens but someone people could relate to. He was, even if they didn't know it yet, a family man with a young child. Maybe it wasn't the image he'd once wanted to project but people could change—*he* had changed as he'd told Lucy more than once recently.

His gaze drifted across the room and he sighed when he saw her look the other way as soon as she realised that he was watching her. Lucy didn't believe he had changed, did she? She didn't believe he was genuine or even just one of the team. She didn't like him, didn't trust him and certainly didn't love him, and it hurt to know that she felt that way.

Connor lifted the cup to his mouth and drank some of the coffee. It was hot and strong but it didn't ease the pain he felt. All his life he'd struggled to prove himself and he had succeeded, too, to a point. His hard work had paid off and in a few years' time he would have attained every goal he had set for himself.

Once upon a time that thought would have filled him with a sense of satisfaction, yet it meant very little to him now. His whole outlook on life had changed, his priorities shifted so far off their original track that it was hard to remember how important they had been. Once he had yearned for success, hungered for the chance to prove his worth and show everyone who had written him off—like his own mother—that they'd been wrong to do so.

Now it no longer mattered so much if he was successful in his career. Now there were more important issues to think about, ones that he had never touched upon before. He had never worried what people had thought of him but he did now. Especially one person. Her opinion mattered more than anyone else's.

Connor put the cup on the table. His hands were shaking and he was afraid he would spill the rest of his coffee. Thoughts seemed to be crowding into his head one after the other until he felt completely overwhelmed. Then slowly one thought rose above all the rest, the one which would make his life mean something: he had to make Lucy believe in him.

Could he do it? Would he succeed? He didn't know. But he had to try or everything he had achieved would be worthless.

CHAPTER TEN

THERE was quite a crowd gathered at Mark and Laura Dawson's house by the time Lucy arrived on Sunday afternoon. Fortunately, the rain had stopped so the barbecue had been able to go ahead as planned. She kissed Laura then handed over the bowl of pasta salad she'd made as her contribution to the proceedings.

'Thank you, but you really shouldn't have gone to all this trouble,' Laura scolded as she took the bowl from her. 'I know what's it like when you have a little one—there's barely enough time to breathe most days!'

'It wasn't any trouble,' Lucy assured her, lifting Izzy out of her buggy. She and Laura had worked together for several years until the other woman had left to have her third child. Laura had found it difficult to combine the demands of her family with her job so she had resigned. Now Lucy grinned at her.

'So where's the lord and master, then?'

'If you mean Mark, he's doing what all men are supposed to do on these occasions—tending the barbie!' Laura laughed as she tickled Izzy under her chin. 'He's being amply assisted by all the other men so that leaves us women free to enjoy ourselves. How about a glass of wine and a nice long gossip for starters?'

'Sounds good to me,' Lucy declared, following her into the kitchen. Laura poured her a glass of wine then whisked Izzy out of her arms. 'Let me have a cuddle while you drink that. My three think they're too old for cuddles now and run a mile when they see me coming.'

Lucy laughed. 'Maybe you should think about having another one if you're feeling broody.'

'Oh, I am, I am! I just haven't told Mark yet.'

'Told me what?' a deep voice demanded.

Lucy turned when she recognised her host's voice, her smile immediately disappearing when she saw the man who was with him. 'What are you doing here?' she demanded, staring at Connor in dismay.

'Mark phoned me yesterday and very kindly invited me along,' he replied smoothly. He put his glass on the table then calmly lifted Izzy out of Laura's arms and kissed her on the cheek.

There was a moment's stunned silence but Lucy could tell what Laura and Mark were thinking from the expressions on their faces. They had obviously worked out that Connor was Izzy's father and Lucy had no idea what she was going to do. In the end it was Laura who came to her rescue with her usual kindness.

'We were just about to have a good old gossip when you two interrupted us. Come along, Lucy. Let's leave them to their own devices and find somewhere quiet where we can put our feet up.'

'What about Izzy...?' Lucy began, but Connor shook his head.

'She'll be fine with me. You go and enjoy yourself, Lucy. You deserve a break.'

The last thing Lucy wanted was to leave Izzy with him but, short of creating a scene, she didn't have any choice. She felt sick with worry as she followed Laura down the garden to the summer house. Most of the other guests had congregated on the patio to avoid the more boggy parts of the lawn, and she waved to them as she passed. She would have to talk to them later, of course, and she felt sicker than ever at the thought of what the main topic of conversation was going to be. She couldn't bear to think that soon everyone would know that Connor was Izzy's father!

'Stop it,' Laura admonished as she opened the summer house door. 'Your secret is safe with me and Mark, so stop worrying yourself to death that we're going to say anything. It's none of our business what you and Connor have decided to do.'

Lucy sank down onto a garden chair. 'It wasn't Connor's decision—it was mine. I didn't want anyone to know that he's Izzy's father.'

'You must have had your reasons so I'm not going to pry and ask you why you decided to keep it quiet.' Laura sat down beside her and patted her hand. 'Although you do realise that people are going to work it out for themselves? I mean, you only have to look at Izzy and you can tell that she's Connor's daughter.'

'Do you think so?' Lucy bit her lip. She had never even considered the idea that people might notice a resemblance between them.

'Yes. She has his hair and his eyes.' Laura smiled gently. 'That's one of the most wonderful things about having kids— they're a sort of composite of both of you.'

'It might be wonderful if you're in a committed relation-ship,' she whispered, fighting back her tears. 'But it's very dif-ferent when the child's father wants nothing to do with you.'

'I certainly didn't get that impression from Connor,' Laura protested. 'His whole face lit up when he saw Izzy!'

'Oh, he's interested in Izzy…or he is at the moment, at any rate. He's definitely not interested in me, though.'

'And that's what really hurts, is it? That's why you didn't tell anyone he was Izzy's father?'

'Yes. I don't want to be an object of pity in everyone's eyes!'

'An object of pity?' Laura repeated, sounding confused.

'Connor dumped me so he could go to Boston to further his precious career. That speaks volumes about his feelings for me, doesn't it?'

'Did he know you were pregnant when he left?' Laura asked, frowning.

'No. I only found out myself after he'd gone.' She shrugged defiantly. 'I decided not to tell him because there didn't seem any point. I wasn't part of his plans for the future, as he had made abundantly clear, so why go creating problems?'

'You didn't tell him!' Laura was obviously shocked by the disclosure, and Lucy flushed.

'No. He found out by accident that I'd had a baby and worked it out for himself that she must be his child. That's why he came back to England and took up this post, in fact— because he wanted access to Izzy.'

'But surely that's a point in his favour? I mean, some men wouldn't have bothered. They'd have considered themselves to have had a lucky escape, but obviously Connor doesn't feel that way.'

'He says that he wants to be a proper father to Izzy, but I'm not sure if he can ever be that. He's always been so focused on his career and I'm terrified that he will end up letting her down because of it.'

'And is that your only concern?' Laura probed gently.

'Isn't it enough?' Lucy countered, because she really didn't want to have to tell her friend all about Dee. A stabbing pain pierced her heart. She still couldn't believe that Connor thought she would be so spiteful as to deny him access to Izzy because he was seeing someone else, yet what other explanation could there be for his strange behaviour regarding Dee?

'If it turns out that you were right then, yes, it is enough. But are you sure that he will let her down? He seemed really smitten to me just now.'

'Oh, he swears he won't, but it's a huge risk, isn't it, Laura? I'm just not sure if I'm prepared to gamble with Izzy's happiness to prove a point.'

'But is it right to deny him access? I mean, Izzy will miss out on such a lot if Connor isn't around while she's growing up. I know that for a fact because Mark has made a huge difference to Robbie's life,' Laura told her, referring to her son from her first marriage who had Down's syndrome. 'Robbie adores Mark and he's really blossomed since we got married. And as for having a brother and a sister now as well—what can I say? If having a father figure has made such a difference to Robbie's life then surely it can only be a good thing for Izzy that Connor wants to be there for her?'

'I suppose you're right but I still can't help worrying,' Lucy admitted.

'Of course you can't! Being a parent is a huge commitment and you want to be sure Connor understands that. I felt exactly the same when Mark asked me to marry him. I didn't want him to end up regretting what he'd taken on, but I needn't have worried.' She glanced across the garden and a smile suddenly lit her face. 'And when you see something like that then it must reassure you.'

Lucy turned to look and felt her heart leap when she saw Connor standing in the midst of a group of people. He had hold of Izzy and even as she watched, she saw him brush the little girl's head with a kiss. It was such a tender expression of his feelings for the child that tears began to trickle down her face.

There was no doubt at all that Connor genuinely loved his daughter so did she really have the right to keep him away from Izzy because of her concerns? Maybe he could never love *her* but that wasn't the point. He loved Izzy and she had to accept that he would do his very best for her otherwise she could end up hurting both of them. She couldn't bear to think that one day, when Izzy grew up, she would blame her for denying her the love and support of her father.

Connor could see the speculation on people's faces when he appeared with Izzy but it had gone too far by that point to worry what they thought. Maybe they would work out that he was her father but he'd be damned if he'd deny her parentage. He glanced round when Sandra appeared at his side, seeing the curiosity in her eyes as she looked from him to the baby.

'I can't believe how much she looks like you, Connor! I suppose it's just a fluke that she has the same colour hair and eyes, but it's really uncanny.'

'These things happen,' he replied neutrally, neither confirming nor denying her suspicions. Whilst he would never deny that he was Izzy's father if someone asked him directly, he wasn't averse to skirting round the issue if it would help Lucy.

His gaze went to the summer house and he felt the blood start to pound inside his head when he saw Lucy walking towards them. Her face was pale but set, and he knew that she had come to some sort of a decision while she'd been talking to Laura. She stopped when she reached him and his blood pounded harder than ever when he saw the plea in her eyes. In that instant he knew that he would do anything she wanted him to do if it meant that she wouldn't get hurt.

'Can I have a word with you?' she said quietly, obviously as aware as he was that everyone was watching them.

'Of course. How about we get ourselves another drink?' He gave her a quick smile, hoping it would reassure her that he wasn't going to cause a scene, but she still looked very strained as she led the way into the house.

Connor followed her into the kitchen and closed the door, not caring what people thought. They could make what they liked of it—his only concern was Lucy and this child they had conceived together. So long as they were safe and happy then nothing else mattered.

He took a deep breath when it hit him that this was how men must have felt since the beginning of time. Looking after the ones you loved was an instinctive part of the male psyche. Women might be the nurturers but men were the protectors, and it was a revelation to suddenly realise his true role in life. Maybe it wasn't PC to think like this, and maybe it smacked of an overload of machismo to state it, but he would lay down his life to protect the woman he loved and their child!

'I'm sorry, Connor. I...I've behaved very badly towards you.'

The softly spoken words took a moment to sink in, but right then Connor had a lot to contend with. He had finally admitted what he had known in his heart all along but had tried to deny: he loved Lucy.

That he loved Izzy as well had never been in any doubt

since the first time he'd seen her, yet it was another revelation to realise that there were so many different shades and nuances to his feelings even though they sprang from the same source. He loved Lucy as a man loved a woman: passionately, hungrily, tenderly, protectively. And he loved Izzy as a father loved a child: selflessly, timelessly, devotedly. The fact that he was capable of feeling so much and so intensely shook him to the core but he had to try and behave like a rational human being because it was what Lucy expected of him. A wave of tenderness washed over him. He would behave any damned way at all if it was what she asked of him!

'You did what you thought was best,' he said, his voice throbbing with emotion.

'Maybe.' She bit her lip and he saw tears well into her eyes. 'But it wasn't fair to you or to Izzy to behave that way.'

'You did your best, Lucy,' he repeated, unbearably moved by her bravery.

This wasn't easy for her either. She still had fears and concerns, still wasn't sure about him, but she had grasped her courage and apologised. He could only admire her for that, and it was another facet to his love, another wonderful feeling to tuck away in his heart.

'I tried, Connor…really I did.'

'And you succeeded.'

All of a sudden he couldn't stand it any more, couldn't bear to watch her suffer when he was supposed to protect her. Maybe he didn't need to fight any dragons at the moment, but protection came in many forms. Lucy needed her tender, gentle heart protected from this agony and he wasn't going to let her down!

He crossed the room in a couple of long strides and pulled

her into his arms, holding her and Izzy close against his heart. If he had his way that was where they would both remain but he mustn't rush things, mustn't get too carried away. He might want to sweep this maiden off her feet and carry her back to his castle but she might not want to go with him…

Just yet.

Afterwards, Connor wasn't sure what had made him act so impulsively. Maybe it had been the promise of things to come, or maybe it had been more prosaic than that. Feeling Lucy's soft curves nestled against him had triggered a chain of reactions: he could feel his blood heating; his breathing quickening; and there was a definite tightening in his groin…

He groaned as he bent and kissed her on the mouth. He knew that if he didn't settle for a kiss he would want something more, and that would be inexcusable with Izzy sitting so trustingly in his arms. Lucy's lips were soft and slightly damp, proof that they weren't the first tears she'd shed that day, and the thought almost tipped him over the edge. However, he had to restrain his feelings and offer her what *she* needed. This was one occasion when passion must wait.

She suddenly reached up and kissed him back, her mouth clinging to his as though she was desperately trying to draw courage from him, and he felt tears spring to his own eyes, too. A great swell of happiness filled him because she could take whatever she wanted from him. Everything he had was hers—including his heart.

When she drew back he couldn't hide how moved he felt and didn't try. 'Thank you,' he said gruffly, because strong emotions took their toll on basic functions.

'I don't know why you're thanking me after what I've done,' she whispered.

'You gave me Izzy,' he said simply. He captured her hand and kissed her soft palm, shuddered, then forced himself to continue. 'No more apologies, Lucy. Please. It isn't necessary.'

'You're right. We have to think about the future now, not the past, don't we?' She held out her arms, smiling when he placed Izzy in them. 'Thank you, too, Connor. For everything.'

He knew what she meant, that she wasn't just thanking him for looking after their daughter but for giving her Izzy in the first place. Lucy was glad that she'd had *his* child, and the thought made him feel ten feet tall as they went back outside together. He wanted to swing from the tree-tops and beat his chest, let loose all those macho feelings which men weren't supposed to feel nowadays. It would have caused one hell of a stir if he had done so, of course, so he behaved with suitable decorum as they rejoined the other guests. However, he could see the knowing looks that were being exchanged and knew that although nothing had been said officially, everyone had filled in the gaps for themselves.

He glanced at Lucy and could tell that she had come to the same conclusion when he saw how strained she looked once more. He sighed as his elation rapidly evaporated. Maybe it had been a bit too soon to start planning for the happily-ever-after. He would have to bide his time, although he wouldn't allow anything deter him from his ultimate goal. One day in the not too distant future, he intended to have both Izzy and Lucy in his life. And this time he wasn't going to let either of them go!

The party broke up shortly after six. Several of the guests were working that night so there was the usual flurry as they got ready to leave. Lucy waited until they'd gone before she took Izzy into the house and put her in her pram. The little girl was worn out after all the excitement and her eyelids started drooping before Lucy had finished strapping her in.

'She's exhausted, isn't she?' Connor said as he came into the hall and crouched down beside them.

'She is. Still, at least she should sleep tonight,' Lucy said lightly, trying to hide how nervous she felt all of a sudden.

Connor had stayed by her side all afternoon long and she knew there wasn't a doubt in anyone's mind now about his relationship to Izzy. There was bound to be a lot of gossip at work once the news broke and she had no idea how he intended to handle it. It might all depend on what that kiss had meant and she still didn't know what to make of it. Had he been merely trying to comfort her? Or had there been more to it than that? The uncertainty was making her feel very on edge.

'Ah, so there you are. We were wondering where you'd got to.'

She glanced round when Laura and Mark appeared, summoning a smile when she saw the concern in their eyes because she didn't want them to think they were in any way to blame for what had gone on that day.

'We're just getting ready to leave. Thank you for having us.' She turned to Connor, deliberately including him so the other couple wouldn't think they were still at loggerheads. 'We really enjoyed it, didn't we?'

'We did, indeed…all three of us.' He stood up and grinned at their hosts. 'In fact, I've made a note to buy myself a barbecue just as soon as I have a garden to put it in. It's obviously the perfect way to wear out the kids and get a bit of peace!'

'I wish. If it was that simple then I'd have Mark firing up our barbie every day of the year!' Laura replied, laughing.

Lucy felt a bit better when she saw the relief on her friend's face. It was obvious that Laura had been worried about any possible repercussions and she couldn't help feeling guilty for unloading her problems onto her. Stepping forward, Lucy gave her a hug. 'It's worth a try, though, don't you think?'

'*Anything* is worth a try,' Laura said softly, looking at her.

Lucy smiled but she knew what Laura had meant and that it had had nothing to do with barbecues either. Laura was telling her that she needed to work things out with Connor. Whilst part of her knew that her friend was right, another part was afraid of where it might lead to. She couldn't pretend that kiss hadn't meant anything to her: it had. But what had it meant to him? What *could* it mean when he was involved with another woman?

The uncertainty gnawed away at her as they finished saying their goodbyes. They left the house and walked up the path. Connor stopped when they reached the lane.

'I'd offer you a lift but I don't have a child seat in my car yet and it isn't safe to hold Izzy on your knee. Maybe you could help me choose one?'

'Of course,' Lucy agreed, doing her best to match his friendly tone. Connor had claimed repeatedly that he and Dee weren't having a relationship…what if he had been telling her the truth all along? It was a tantalising thought, yet she was afraid to believe it. She didn't think she could face another major disappointment in her life.

'Uh-oh. Here we go again.'

She glanced up as he drew her attention to the fact that it had started raining again. 'Oh, dear! It looks as though we're in for another downpour, doesn't it?' she exclaimed, bending down to retrieve the pram cover from the shopping tray.

'You're going to get soaked,' Connor said worriedly, looking up at the sky. 'Don't you at least have an umbrella with you?'

'Yes, but it's virtually impossible to hold an umbrella and push a pram,' she explained, fastening the rain cover in place. Izzy was fast asleep and she didn't stir when Lucy finished by pulling up the hood. 'I'm going to make a dash for it,' she said, turning to Connor. 'I'll see you at work tomorrow.'

'I'm not letting you walk home and get soaked,' he said firmly, bending down to take the umbrella out of the tray. He unfurled it then held it over her. 'I'll walk you home then come back for my car.'

'Oh, no, really, it isn't necessary.'

'Of course it is.' He suddenly grinned at her, his green eyes sparkling with laughter and something that made her breath catch. She had never expected to see such tenderness in his eyes when he looked at her. 'Now we can stand here all night and argue about it, but I'm going to win in the end, Lucy. Whether you like it or not, I'm going to play the perfect gentleman and walk you home!'

Lucy huffed out a sigh but it was purely for show. All her objections seemed to have melted away. She knew it was silly to let a look affect her, but add it to that kiss and she couldn't help it. Was it possible that Connor actually cared about her?

'If that's what you want to do,' she said, setting off up the lane because she couldn't stand there while thoughts like that tormented her.

'It is.'

Connor didn't say anything else as he strode along beside her and she was glad. She had enough on her mind without having to make conversation as well. It took them a good ten minutes to reach her flat and by that time the rain was hammering down. Although the umbrella had sheltered her from the worst of the downpour, Connor was soaked through. As she unlocked her front door, she realised that the very least she could do was to invite him in so he could wait until the rain eased off.

'You'd better come in,' she said, manoeuvring the buggy into the tiny hallway. 'The rain should slacken off soon so there's no point getting another soaking, is there?'

'I'm not sure if I could get any wetter,' he said wryly. 'I don't think I was this wet after I dived into the river last week, in fact!'

Lucy smiled at that. 'You don't seem to have had much luck lately, do you?'

'Oh, I wouldn't say that.' He closed the door and her breath caught when he turned to face her. She couldn't recall seeing such yearning on anyone's face before.

'I think fortune has been smiling on me recently, Lucy. I feel like the luckiest man alive because I have everything any man could dream of having.'

CHAPTER ELEVEN

CONNOR knew he shouldn't have said that. It was too soon. He'd already decided that he would bide his time yet seeing Lucy standing there had been too big a temptation. She looked so beautiful with her hair curling damply around her face that he would have needed a heart of stone not to have felt anything. Now all he needed to do was to convince her that he was serious.

'Lucy, I know this might be—'

He stopped when Izzy suddenly woke up and started crying. Lucy hurriedly bent down and unfastened the rain cover.

'I'd better get her out of there before she screams the place down,' she said, her voice quavering.

'Of course.' Connor sighed. It was obvious that she was relieved to have an excuse not to listen to him. Just for a moment he found himself wondering if he was mad to hope that he could get her back. Lucy may have loved him in the past but she hadn't given him any reason to think that she still loved him now. She might be glad that she'd had Izzy but it didn't mean that she wanted him as well.

It was a sobering thought and one which he knew that he had to consider very carefully. Even though he loved her with all his heart, he wouldn't try to force her into a relationship she no longer wanted. She had to love him too for it to mean anything, and the thought that she might never feel that way about him again filled him with anguish. *He* was the one who had put his career before everything else—including her. And it was *his* fault if she had stopped loving him!

'I'm going to change Izzy and put her in her cot. There's fresh towels in the bathroom if you want to dry yourself off.'

'Thanks.' Connor forced his thoughts to the darkest reaches of his mind because he couldn't deal with them right then. Knowing the blame lay squarely with him was more than he could bear. He dredged up a smile. 'I'll put the kettle on after I've finished. What would you prefer—tea or coffee?'

'I don't mind—you choose.'

She gave him a quick and decidedly impersonal smile as she disappeared into the bedroom, and his sagging spirits sagged even more. That she could behave that way towards him just seemed to confirm his fears. Lucy no longer loved him and it was all his fault. He had thrown away his chance of happiness for the sake of his career and it was hard to deal with the thought of how different his life might have been now if he'd realised sooner what was really important.

The thought hung over him like a cloud as he went into the bathroom. His sweater was soaked so he took it off and dropped it in the bath, then towelled his hair. His shirt was damp but he left it on, preferring not to parade around the flat half-naked. He doubted if Lucy would take kindly to him making himself at home!

It was another deflating thought so he went into the kitchen and switched on the kettle rather than dwell on it. By the time Lucy appeared he had a pot of coffee ready and waiting.

'I made coffee,' he told her, glancing round.

'Oh…right. Fine.'

'I could make some tea if you'd prefer it,' he suggested, because she hadn't sounded very enthusiastic about the coffee.

'No, coffee's fine,' she said, avoiding his eyes.

Connor frowned as he put the pot on the table. She looked so uncomfortable that he couldn't help wondering what was wrong…unless she didn't want him there and didn't know how to ask him to leave?

'Look, Lucy, you only have to say the word and I'll go.'

'Of course I don't want you to leave! Why should I?'

'You tell me.' He shrugged. 'You just look a bit…well, uptight, I suppose, is the best way to describe it.'

'You're imagining things,' she said sharply, walking over to the fridge. She took out a carton of milk then edged around him to get the milk jug, which was on the top shelf close to where he was standing.

'Here, let me get that for you,' he offered. Turning round, he went to take it off the shelf then froze when his hand accidentally brushed against hers as she reached for it as well.

Connor breathed in sharply when he felt a surge of energy race up his arm. It felt as though he had poked his fingers into a live electrical socket. He glanced at Lucy and could tell that she had felt it, too. The question now was what should he do?

Lucy didn't say a word when he handed her the jug but he could see that she was trembling as she placed it on the worktop. She didn't look at him as she filled it with milk and the fact that she couldn't even bear to look at him was more than he could stand.

'I wish I could put things right, Lucy, but I can't. I can't turn back the clock, no matter how much I might want to do so.'

'I know. Even if we could go back, there's nothing to go back for, is there?'

The emptiness in her voice tore at his heart. 'Don't say that! We were good together, Lucy—you know we were.'

'Do I?' She smiled sadly. 'I used to think we were but I was wrong. If we were so good together then why did you leave me?'

'Because I thought it was what I wanted. I honestly believed it was the best thing I could do—for you as well as for me.'

'So you were trying to help me by leaving?' She laughed and it was all he could do not to sweep her into his arms when he heard the hurt in her voice. 'Well, I have to say that I've never thought about it that way before. Silly me. I thought you left to further your career, but obviously I was mistaken.'

'You weren't mistaken. That was all part and parcel of it,' he grated out. 'I had a plan, you see, goals that I'd set for myself, and working in America was one of them.'

He ran his hands through his hair, wishing he could explain how hard it had been to stick to those plans he'd made. He had wanted to stay with her so desperately but even if he told her that now, why should she believe him? Words were easy, as he knew to his cost—actions said far more. And his actions at the time had convinced her how little he had cared about her. No wonder she found it impossible to believe in him!

The thought filled him with dread and he took a step towards her but she held up her hand. 'No! Whatever you're planning on doing, please, don't. I don't want you to try and persuade me that what you did was right for me. I remember how I felt after you left and I'm never, *ever* going to feel that way again.'

'It was hard for me, too, Lucy,' he said, his voice catching as he remembered all the nights he had lain awake, wishing she had been there beside him. If only he'd been honest with himself at the time then things might have been very different now, but he'd been afraid to admit to his feelings in case they had got in the way of his goals. And it was the bitterest punishment of all to know that he had brought this on himself.

'I didn't just fly off to Boston and forget all about you,' he said quietly.

'Maybe not, but you didn't try to contact me, did you? If it was that hard to leave then the very least I would have expected was that you would have phoned me.'

'I thought about it,' he admitted. 'But each time I decided it wouldn't be fair to you.'

'Because you weren't prepared to put our relationship first and your career second?'

'Yes.' He sighed wearily. It was a terrible admission to make, but he wouldn't lie to her. 'I've always put my career first and I thought I always would. But not now. I've realised now that there are more important things in life than being successful.'

'Meaning Izzy?'

'Yes, Izzy…and you.' He looked at her then and felt his heart jolt when he saw the surprise in her eyes. He'd obviously shocked her by that admission so would she be prepared to listen to him now? It was just the tiniest glimmer of hope but it was enough to spur him on.

He captured her hands and held them tightly, needing to convince her that he was telling the truth. 'You mean such a lot to me, too, Lucy. It isn't just Izzy who has changed my life but being with you again. It's made me realise how much I lost when I went away.'

'Please, don't say that if you don't mean it,' she whispered, her eyes brimming with tears. 'I don't think I could bear it if you hurt me again.'

'I will never, ever hurt you again,' he said thickly.

'Promise?'

'On my life.'

The words were barely out of his mouth before he was reaching for her. He knew he should have waited but he had to convince her that he was sincere and this was the best way he knew. Their mouths met in a kiss which should have felt clumsy because of its lack of finesse yet he groaned when he felt the passion it held. There was no way that he could hold back now when he wanted her so much but, amazingly, Lucy didn't seem to want him to.

They kissed each other with a hunger that stemmed from desperation. Connor knew that he was trying to show her how much he loved her through his actions in case words weren't enough. People had told him things and not meant them, but this kiss would tell her everything he needed it to.

She meant the whole world to him because she had given him the promise of a future he had never dreamt of. Home and family was a concept he had no experience of, but Lucy had shown him how wonderful it could be. If he could have her and Izzy then he wouldn't want anything else: his life would be complete.

The thought was unbearably moving and his lips gentled, passion turning to tenderness in the blink of an eye. Where once he would have tried to guard his emotions, now he wanted to share them with her—wanted her to know how deeply he felt. The kiss was like nothing he had experienced before because this time he held nothing back. He laid bare his heart and his soul and everything he was, and she responded with an openness that filled him with joy. Even after the way he had hurt her, she still trusted him!

His hands were shaking as he swept her into his arms and carried her into the sitting-room and it was another first. He'd always been a confident lover in the past, but this was different. He had never loved this deeply before, never needed to prove his worth as a man and not just his prowess as a lover, but he needed to do so now. He wanted Lucy to love him for what he was—all his bad points as well as the good—and that made him feel more than a little afraid. But if she could trust him after what he had done to her, then he most definitely could trust her!

He laid her on the sofa then knelt on the floor beside her and kissed her mouth, her jaw, her cheeks. Her skin was warm and flushed, slightly damp from her tears, and his desire grew with each kiss. He wanted to brand her with his lips, make her his until eternity, and it was such an elemental feeling that he found himself smiling in amazement. Another day like this and he would turn into a real caveman!

'What are you smiling about?' she whispered.

'Me. I'm turning into a caveman.' He kissed her again, his lips skating down the gentle slope of her nose and hovering just above her mouth so that he could taste the sweetness of her breath when she laughed.

'Oh, I *see*. So does that mean you're going to drag me back to your cave and have your wicked way with me?'

'I might—if I had a cave to drag you back to.' His mouth moved lower, his lips barely brushing hers, yet he could feel the contact in every pore in his body. He breathed in deeply, forcing his senses to quieten down while he savoured the moment. It had been a long time since he'd been this close to her and he didn't want to rush things when he could take his time…

His mouth seemed to move of its own volition, swooping down to steal a kiss, making a mockery of his plans, and he groaned. How could he be patient when he wanted her so much that every bit of him ached?

The kiss ran on and on so that they were both breathless when he finally managed to prise himself away from her. 'See what I mean?' he muttered. 'You make me come over all macho even when I don't intend to.'

'Oh, so it's my fault, is it?' She cocked a silky brow at him and he laughed, loving the fact that she felt confident enough to tease him.

'Of course it is!'

'In that case, maybe we should go back to the kitchen and have that coffee,' she suggested sweetly. 'I wouldn't like to make you do anything else against your will.'

'You won't,' he grated a second before his mouth claimed hers again.

Lucy twined her arms around his neck and kissed him back, her lips opening so that he could deepen the kiss, and Connor felt his blood pressure shoot sky high. He knew there wasn't a hope of him calling a halt if he let this continue, and knew too that he had to make sure she understood that. He might want to make love to her more than he wanted air to breathe, but it had to be her decision as well, not just his.

He forced himself away from her and looked into her eyes. 'If you want me to stop then say so now. I want to make love with you, Lucy, but it has to be what you want, too.'

'It is.' Reaching up, she kissed him on the mouth and there was no trace of doubt in her voice. 'I want you, Connor. Just as much.'

'Thank you.' His voice shook but he didn't care. He didn't

care about anything apart from the fact that he had won her back. When he started to unbutton her blouse, he could feel every nerve in his body go taut with anticipation. One button slid out and a second but then he had to stop because he was trembling uncontrollably.

'Let me do it,' she said, pushing his hands aside.

Connor sank back on his heels as he watched her unfasten her blouse. She came to the last button and undid that too then paused. Her eyes were huge when she looked at him and he could see the invitation they held, yet he couldn't make himself respond to it. He wanted to strip away the blouse, touch her, caress her, so much that it hurt, yet all the strength seemed to have seeped out of his muscles—and he couldn't do a damned thing about it!

'I can't,' he gritted out from between clenched teeth.

'You mean you don't want to…?'

'No, I mean that I do. Too much!'

Understanding crossed her face as she leant over and kissed him. 'Then I'll help you.'

She sat up and shimmied out of the blouse, tossing it over the back of the sofa with a flourish that made him moan with frustration.

Her hands went to the fastening on her bra as she looked at him with a question in her eyes, and somehow he managed to nod. She undid the hooks then it too went sailing over the back of the sofa. All she had on now was a pair of jeans—tight jeans which fitted her curves like a second skin—and he groaned.

'This is sheer bloody torture,' he muttered, trying—and failing—to make himself move.

'Is it? Oh, dear.' She leant towards him so that her breasts brushed against his chest and all the air rushed out of his body when he felt her nipples harden.

'Torture,' he repeated, because finding another way to describe the way he was feeling was beyond his capabilities right then. His body was in agony—desperate for her!

'I don't know what we can do about it, do you?' She moved closer still, put her arms around him, held him so he could feel every soft, delectable inch, and all of a sudden power came surging back to him. Connor let out a gasp of relief as he wrapped his arms around her.

'I think you might just have found the solution!'

He kissed her hungrily then stripped off her jeans and panties. There was a burning hunger building inside him, an urgency that wouldn't be quelled, and he didn't try. He swore softly when he had to waste more precious seconds ridding himself of his own clothing because he could tell that she was as impatient as he was. Her arms were already reaching up to him as he lowered himself down to her and they closed around him as though they would never let him go again.

They made love right there on the sofa and it was the most moving experience of his life. What started as an outlet for their passion turned into so much more. Lucy had been hurt and he tried to heal her pain, yet in doing so he found to his amazement that he healed a lot of his own pain as well.

Tears ran down his cheeks as the memories of his childhood started to fade. He had carried the burden for such a long time yet now it felt as though it had been lifted off him. Maybe his mother hadn't been able to love him but Lucy could. She would love and care for him and knowing that was the most wonderful gift she could have given him…apart from Izzy.

That she had given him a child too seemed too much, and he cried with joy as well as relief. He had been given more than any man had the right to expect and he would always be grateful to her for that, always love her, always care for her. And in return he would give her everything he had—his heart, his soul, his life. She and Izzy were his whole world now, and he wanted to be their whole world, too.

Lucy hadn't believed that she could ever feel so happy. When she and Connor had been together before, part of her had always held back. She had known that he would leave her and her pleasure had been tinged with sadness, but not any more. She was happy from the top of her head to the tips of her toes—and every tiny bit in between!—and she couldn't stop smiling.

'You, Staff Nurse Adams, are grinning like the proverbial Cheshire cat.' Connor grinned himself as he propped himself up on his elbow, and she laughed.

'Are you complaining?'

'Nope. I most certainly am not.' He kissed her softly on the mouth then smiled at her with a world of tenderness in his eyes. 'I love seeing you smile, Lucy. I don't ever want you to feel sad again.'

'Far be it from me to tempt fate but I must say that it seems highly unlikely at this moment.' She kissed him on the mouth, then on the nose and eyelids, because it was so wonderful to have that right restored to her. She could kiss him whenever and wherever she chose, and the thought made her grin all the more.

'Hmm! Dare I ask what you're thinking about?'

'Of course you can ask. It doesn't mean that I have to tell

you, of course,' she retorted, earning herself another kiss as a punishment…or maybe as a reward.

The kiss was well on its way to turning into something more when there was a familiar buzzing sound from somewhere on the floor. Lucy groaned as she flopped back against the cushions. 'Is that what I think it is?'

''Fraid so.' Connor sighed as he reached for his jeans and hunted his pager out of the pocket. He checked the display then sat up. 'It's the hospital…surprise, surprise. I'm sorry, Lucy, but I can't ignore it.'

'It's all right,' she assured him, because it was true. Now that they seemed to have cleared everything up, she felt far more relaxed about his job. There would be times when his work would have to come first, but she understood that. As long as she knew that he would always try to make her and Izzy his main priority, she didn't feel so threatened, and it was a relief to have the fear lifted off her.

She kissed him quickly then got up, knowing that it wasn't the right time to explain her feelings to him. He needed to respond to the call so she went into the bedroom for her robe while he phoned the hospital. He was already dressed when she came back and she frowned when she saw how grim he looked.

'What's happened?'

'Alan Johnson and Amy Marshall have gone missing. Bea's informed Security and they're searching the hospital for them,' he explained, zipping up his jeans. 'Alan's case worker has been informed as well as Amy's parents so I need to go in and talk to them.'

'Where on earth have they gone?'

'I've no idea but there's going to be a hell of stink if we don't find them soon.' He strode to the door then paused and she could see the uncertainty in his eyes. 'I'm sorry, Lucy. There's such a lot of things we need to talk about…'

'It can wait.' She smiled at him, wanting to reassure him that he had no reason to worry. 'I'm not going anywhere—are you?'

'No.' An expression of relief lit his face as he came back and kissed her quickly on the mouth. He rested his forehead against hers for a moment and she felt the tremor that ran through him. 'I'm not going to make the same mistake twice.'

Lucy smiled as he let her go and hurried out of the flat. Maybe it hadn't been an actual declaration of love but it had been as good as one. Connor had promised that he wasn't going to leave her again and she knew that he had meant it, too.

She tidied up, took her discarded clothes into the kitchen and popped them in the washing machine, then headed to the bathroom for a shower. Connor had forgotten to take his sweater with him and she smiled as she hung it on the towel rail because it seemed like an omen for the future. His clothes and hers would soon be sharing drawer space…

Wouldn't they?

She paused, wondering where that doubt had appeared from. Everything that had happened in the past hour had proved that he cared about her so why should she start worrying about the future? Maybe he hadn't told her that he loved her yet, but that would come later…

Wouldn't it?

She quickly turned on the shower. It was stupid to let one doubt turn into a dozen. Either she trusted him or she didn't, and she'd already decided which it was. Connor could *never* have made love to her like that if he hadn't loved her!

She stepped under the water, hoping the spray would wash away any more foolish ideas. Admittedly, there were a few things they needed to sort out, like his involvement with Dee, for instance, but she was confident there was an innocent explanation for that. The whole basis of love was trust and she wasn't going to ruin things by not trusting him.

CHAPTER TWELVE

'HAVE you checked the CCTV footage? I thought all the exits were supposed to be monitored.'

Connor tried to curb his impatience as the head of the security unit explained that there was no sign of the children leaving the building on the video tapes. It was two hours since Amy and Alan had disappeared and the longer they were gone, the greater the danger they could be in.

'Then we have to assume they are still inside the hospital. I'll be here for the rest of the night so make sure you phone me as soon as you hear anything, please.'

He put the phone back on its rest then turned to Bea and sighed. 'Nothing. There's no sign of the kids leaving the building so they must still be here somewhere. I suppose that's something to be grateful for.'

'But where are they? I mean, how can two kids just disappear?'

'I wish I knew,' he said grimly. He really could have done without this happening right now. He needed to spend more time with Lucy and make sure they had cleared up all the misunderstandings that had arisen recently. The thought that he might have put their reconciliation in jeopardy made him go cold until he remembered what she'd said to him before he'd left. She trusted in him now, and knew that he wouldn't let her down again.

The thought calmed him and he smiled at Bea. 'Look, Bea, you've got to stop blaming yourself. Those kids obviously planned this and they were just waiting for the right moment to make their escape.'

'I know that! But I'm supposed to be in charge of this ward so it's my fault that they've gone missing. I'll never forgive myself if anything happens to them—'

'Nothing is going to happen to them,' Connor said firmly. 'They haven't left the building so they can't have gone far. The security guys will find them—you'll see.'

'I hope so.'

Bea gave him a tight smile as she left the office. Connor followed her out but instead of going back to the ward, he made his way to the relatives' room. Amy's parents had arrived shortly after he had got there and he wasn't looking forward to speaking to them.

In the event, the meeting turned out to be every bit as fraught as he'd feared. Whilst he could appreciate that any parent would be upset in such circumstances, Amy's parents seemed more concerned about suing the hospital trust for negligence than finding out where their daughter had gone. When Connor left them a short time later, he found it hard to hide his disgust. If they had put as much effort into being good parents as they put into making money then Amy might not have run away.

It made him see why Lucy had been so worried about his involvement in Izzy's life. There could be no half-measures when you were a parent. You had to put your child first and everything else second, and he smiled as he walked along the corridor. Once that idea would have been anathema to him but now it filled him with a real sense of purpose. He couldn't think of anything he wanted to do more than make sure his precious little girl was loved and cherished…

Apart from making sure that her mother was loved and cherished, too!

There was still no sign of the missing children when Lucy arrived at work the following morning. The security team had searched the whole of the hospital to no avail. The police had been called in and they were taking statements from all the staff who'd been on duty the previous night.

Lucy waited outside the office until Bea had finished giving her statement. She could see how upset the other woman looked after the police had left. 'Still no news?' she asked as she went into the room.

'Nothing. I just don't know where they've got to. The whole building has been searched and there's no sign of them.'

Lucy sighed. 'It isn't your fault, Bea. You weren't to know they were planning this.'

'That's what Connor said.' Bea managed to smile. 'I thought I'd be in for a real rollicking but he was lovely about it. He's changed such a lot, hasn't he? Maybe Tom is right and it's all down to the power of love. If that's the case then the sooner Connor and Dee make it official the better is all I can say!'

'You never know.'

Lucy managed to smile but she couldn't pretend the comment hadn't hurt. Obviously, people still believed that Connor and Dee were an item and it was upsetting to know that after what had happened the night before. She made up her mind to talk to him about it as soon as she could. They needed to put things right before it caused any more confusion. Once everyone found out that Connor was Izzy's father, the rumour-mongers were going to have a field day!

There was no time to speak to him then, unfortunately. Having the police there had set everything back and there were the breakfasts to sort out and obs to be checked. Lucy did the obs with Sandra while Mary Morris, one of their part-time staff, organised the breakfasts. There was nobody in the high-dependency unit so that meant one less task to be done, but there was still a lot of work to get through before the ward round commenced.

Lucy could feel her excitement mounting as the time when she would see Connor again drew nearer. It would have been wonderful if he could have spent the night with her but she understood why he'd had to leave. A situation like this was something out of the ordinary and, as the head of the department, he needed to take charge. However, even though she understood that, she couldn't help feeling disappointed when Martin arrived with the team and informed her that Connor wouldn't be joining them. Apparently, he was closeted with the trust's lawyers and had asked Martin to take over from him.

Lucy led them to the first bed but she saw the look that Amanda and Tom exchanged and knew what they were thinking. They must have heard the rumours about Connor and Izzy and probably had assumed that he was avoiding her. Maybe they thought that he was embarrassed at the thought of people knowing he was Izzy's father when he was, reportedly, having a relationship with another woman?

Lucy longed to set them straight but she didn't feel it was her place. It would be better coming from Connor. However, the sooner this was sorted out, the happier she would be. She certainly didn't want everyone to think that he was in love with another woman when it wasn't true!

Connor was glad to escape after his meeting with the lawyers. It had been a very tense affair and he knew there were going to be repercussions in the coming months. Once upon a time the thought that his career might have been damaged would have worried him, but he was more concerned about the missing children now. Where had they gone? And why hadn't they been found if they were still inside the building?

He went back to the paediatric unit, feeling his spirits lift as he stepped out of the lift. It was nearly lunchtime and with a bit of luck he might be able to persuade Lucy to join him for an impromptu picnic in his office. They could buy sandwiches from the canteen and enjoy some time alone together. It might not be that long since he'd seen her last, but if he didn't see her soon then he might not survive!

He was just passing the office when he heard Dee calling him so he stopped and waited for her to catch up with him. 'I didn't know you were working today,' he said, smiling at her.

'I'm not. I just wanted a word with you but I'm not sure if now is a good time.' She pulled a face. 'I just met Sandra and she told me about the missing kids.'

'It's a real worry,' Connor agreed.

'It is. Anyway, I can tell that you're busy so I'll leave it for now.'

'Hang on!' He held up his hand when she started to walk away. 'What did you want to see me about?'

'It's OK. You've more important things to think about than my problems.' She grinned at him. 'A little bird told me that you might have been keeping a secret from us.'

He rolled his eyes. 'That little bird isn't called Sandra, by any chance?' He shook his head when Dee laughed. 'I might have known she'd be the one to tell everyone, not that it matters, of course.'

'So it's true, then? Lucy and you have a daughter?'

'Yes.' He couldn't help smiling. 'I should have bought some cigars and handed them round. It isn't every day you can announce that you're a father!'

'Well, I think it's wonderful news, Connor, really I do,' she insisted. However, he saw her mouth tremble when she tried to smile at him and realised how hard it must be for her to congratulate him in the circumstances.

'How are things between you and Mike?' he asked gently.

'Confusing.' She sighed. 'That's what I wanted to talk to you about. I need some advice and I need it to be impartial, too. There's no point talking to my parents because they're too involved.'

'Then let's go into the office while you tell me what's happened,' he said, opening the door.

Dee didn't argue as she followed him into the room. It was obvious that she was desperate to talk to him. She didn't even stop to close the door before she launched right in. 'Mike flew over to England last week to see me. He's come up with an idea but I'm not sure how I feel about it.'

'So what has he suggested?' Connor asked, leaning against the desk.

'That we think about egg donation to allow us to have a family.'

'And you hate the idea?'

'No, it's not that. I just don't know if it will work...' She tailed off unhappily, and he frowned.

'You're afraid the child will resent it when he or she finds out that you used a donor?'

'Well, obviously that is a concern, but it's more to do with how I'm going to feel after the baby is born.' She sighed. 'It won't be my biological child, will it, so how can I be sure that I'll love it?'

'You can't be sure of that, Dee,' he said gently. 'But there again you can't be sure that you would love your own child either.'

He smiled sadly when she looked at him in astonishment. Even though he never discussed his own circumstances, he knew it could help her make up her mind if he told her. 'My mother had me taken into care when I was a child. My father died when I was a baby and she met someone else when I was about six years old and he didn't want me around.' He shrugged. 'She chose him over me.'

'But that's awful!' Dee exclaimed. 'How could she have done that?'

'I don't know.' Connor wasn't sure why he wanted to convince her the plan could work. Maybe it was because he'd discovered how wonderful it was to be a father. It seemed such a shame that two people as kind and as caring as Mike and Dee might never have the chance to be parents.

'Think about it, Dee. You desperately want a baby and you can't have one, so this could be the ideal solution. After all, this child's father would be the man you love, so how could you *not* love it as well?'

'That's wonderful news… Yes, I'll tell Dr Mackenzie immediately.'

Lucy sighed with relief as she hung up the phone. Alan and

Amy had been found hiding in the boiler room, none the worse for their adventures, apparently. They were being returned to the ward so now all she had to do was to tell Connor.

She hurried along the corridor, wondering if she should page him in case he was still with the lawyers. The sooner he knew about this, the sooner everything could get back to normal. She went to the desk, glancing round when Sandra appeared.

'They've found the children so I'm just paging Connor to tell him the good news.'

'There's no need to page him. I just saw him and Dee going into the office.'

'Did you?' Lucy dropped the receiver onto its rest, feeling her heart start to pound. 'Is Dee supposed to be working today?' she said as calmly as she could.

'I don't think so. She usually only works if we need cover for the high-dependency unit, doesn't she?' Sandra shrugged. 'She probably came in to see Connor—'

Sandra broke off abruptly and Lucy saw the embarrassed colour run up her face. It was obvious that her friend thought she had said something wrong but there was no need for her to worry, Lucy told herself sternly. Connor had proved last night that he couldn't possibly be interested in Dee.

'I'll go along to the office and tell him what's happened, then. Can you make a start on the lunches? I won't be long.'

She hurried away before Sandra could say anything else. The office door was open and she paused, wondering if she should knock before she went in. She wouldn't like to interrupt them if they were having a private conversation…

'Think about it, Dee. You desperately want a baby and you can't have one, so this could be the ideal solution. After all, this child's father would be the man you love, so how could you *not* love it as well?'

Lucy reeled back in shock when she heard Connor speak. She heard Dee say something to him in reply but she couldn't understand the words—it was too difficult to make sense of them. Was Connor trying to persuade Dee to accept Izzy? Did he see Izzy as an integral part of *their* future together? She didn't want to believe it but what else could she think after hearing that?

You desperately want a baby and you can't have one...this child's father would be the man you love...

Snatches of the conversation rushed back to her as she made her way back along the corridor. Connor wanted Izzy for *Dee's* sake and that was why he had come back to England. Was that it? He wanted their daughter to fill the gap in Dee's life?

It explained so much that hadn't made sense before. He had never been interested in having a family with Lucy, had never put anything before his career when he had been with her, but now he was prepared to make any sacrifice so long as the woman he loved was happy.

Lucy put her hand over her mouth as sickness welled into her throat. She only just made it to the bathroom before she threw up. She leant against the wall as a wave of revulsion swept over her. Connor had hurt her once before but it was nothing compared to what he'd done to her now. He had used Izzy for his own purposes and she would never forgive him for that until the day she died.

Connor went straight to the ward after Dee had left but there was no sign of Lucy. Sandra was in the dayroom, helping the children with their lunch, so he popped his head round the door.

'Where's Lucy?'

'I thought she'd gone to the office to find you,' Sandra told him in surprise.

'Did she?' He glanced over his shoulder but there was no way that he could have missed seeing Lucy on his way there.

'Maybe she got called away,' Sandra suggested. 'They might have wanted her to go downstairs to see Amy and Alan.'

'You mean they've been found!'

'Yes, sorry. I forgot that Lucy hasn't spoken to you yet. They found them in the boiler room, apparently.'

'Thank heavens for that!' He looked round when he heard voices and saw two decidedly dejected youngsters being shepherded back to the ward. 'Here they come now. I'll have a word with them first then speak to Amy's parents and Alan's social worker. If you see Lucy, will you tell her that I'll catch up with her later?'

He ushered the children into the office so he could talk to them in private. He wanted to get to the bottom of why they had run away because he didn't want it happening again. One of the trust's lawyers was with them and he insisted on joining them, obviously concerned about the impact their disappearance could have on the hospital's reputation.

'OK, guys, sit yourselves down and tell me what you were up to. You must have realised that a lot of people would be extremely worried about you so why did you do it?'

'Nobody's worried about me,' Alan muttered. 'They don't care what happens to me at that place. That's why I never want to go back there!'

'It's the same for me,' Amy said, tears rolling down her face. 'My parents are too busy to worry about me. I'm just a nuisance to them. The only thing they care about is how much money they make.'

Connor sighed. They were too very unhappy kids but he had to make them understand the danger they'd put themselves in. 'I know you thought you had a genuine reason for running away but what if something had happened to you? The staff on this ward would have been blamed and that wouldn't have been fair to them, would it?'

They looked so downcast at the idea that he didn't have the heart to chastise them any more. 'I want you both to promise me that you won't do anything like this again.'

They gave him their word so he took them back to the ward and went to talk to the Marshalls and Alan's social worker. Mr and Mrs Marshall were very indignant when he relayed what Amy had said, and threatened to sue him if he repeated the comments to anyone else, but Connor didn't back down. As he pointed out to them, their daughter was unhappy enough at home to abuse inhalants, and so unhappy that she'd decided to run away rather than go back there.

He pulled no punches when it came to the treatment Alan had received at the care home either. He told the social worker that standards there needed to be improved and that he intended to see that they were. The trust's lawyer was almost apoplectic by the time he'd finished but Connor didn't care. Someone needed to stand up for these kids and he was just the person to do it.

He went back to the ward after the meeting ended and examined the children. They seemed none the worse for their exploits so he asked Sandra to make sure they had their lunch and to call him immediately if she was worried about them.

There was still no sign of Lucy when he left and he sighed as he made his way to the lift. So much for his plans to spend a little quality time with her! He had a finance meeting that afternoon so it would be the end of the day before he could catch up with her now. As he got into the lift, he realised that the time couldn't come soon enough. Every second he spent away from her was a second wasted.

CHAPTER THIRTEEN

LUCY had no idea how she got through the day. The horror of discovering how Connor had tricked her made her feel ill. She didn't want to believe that he could have treated her so badly but what else was she supposed to think after overhearing what he'd said to Dee? He wanted Izzy for Dee's sake, and he was prepared to do whatever it took to achieve his objective—including sleeping with her.

'You look really awful, Lucy. Don't you feel well?'

Lucy dredged up a smile when Sandra accosted her as she was leaving the ward. 'I've got a headache.'

'Oh, poor you!' Sandra exclaimed. 'Mind you, it's no wonder after what's been happening recently, is it?'

Lucy sighed when she saw the curiosity on her friend's face. 'If you mean Connor then why don't you come out and say so?'

'Because I was trying to be tactful, of course.' Sandra grinned at her. 'You're a dark horse, Lucy. I would never have guessed that he was Izzy's father in a million years!'

Lucy smiled thinly. It wasn't the most tactful comment, although no doubt a lot of other people felt that way: they couldn't understand what Connor had seen in her. 'You weren't supposed to guess. That's the reason I kept quiet about it.'

'Did Connor know about Izzy before he came back here?' Sandra asked inquisitively.

'Yes, he knew.' And he had made his plans accordingly, she thought, although she didn't say so, of course.

Fortunately, the office phone started ringing so she made her escape but she knew how awkward it was going to be from now on, working with Connor. Now that she understood why he had come back to England, she wasn't sure if she could bear to be around him. He had used her but if he thought he was going to use their daughter, he was mistaken! Izzy wasn't a commodity. She couldn't be used to fill the hole in Dee's life. Even though Lucy felt sorry for Dee, she wouldn't allow her daughter to be made use of that way. And she intended to make that perfectly clear to Connor as soon as she saw him.

There was no time to go in search of him then, though. The phone call was from A and E to say that they had ten-year-old twin boys who needed admitting. Nicholas and Simon Gentry had been rushed into hospital after suffering severe asthma attacks. The family was on holiday in the area so their GP had been contacted and he had agreed to fax through their notes. Although both boys were stable now, their sats were down so the A and E consultant had decided to keep them in overnight.

Lucy got them settled in neighbouring beds then paged Connor. Their mother had accompanied them to the ward and she looked very shaky when Lucy showed her to the relatives' room.

'I don't what set them off today. I checked their air flow this morning as I always do and they were fine. I know Nicholas had a bit of cold last week but Simon didn't catch it,' Mrs Gentry explained worriedly.

'Do you know what tends to trigger their attacks?' Lucy asked.

'Anything and everything!' Mrs Gentry sank down onto a chair. 'It started off with cat hair…we had a cat when they were born, you see, but we had to have her rehomed because the boys were wheezing all the time. The attacks stopped for a while but they started off again and this time our GP said that they might be allergic to house dust so we got rid of all the carpets and had wooden floors laid.'

'Did that help?' Lucy asked sympathetically.

'Yes. But then they started nursery school and the whole cycle began again—I was beside myself with worry every time I took them to school!'

'It must have been very difficult for you.'

'It's been a nightmare and it still is. I'm terrified that something is going to happen to them both…'

Lucy patted her shoulder when the poor woman started to cry. She looked up when Mary knocked on the door to tell her that Connor had arrived. She asked Mary to stay with Mrs Gentry and left the room, steeling herself as she made her way to the office. She didn't intend to have a row with him here and run the risk of anyone hearing what she said. What she wanted to say to him needed to be said in private.

'Hi! I believe you wanted me?'

Her heart ached when he greeted her with a warm smile. If she hadn't overheard that conversation then she would have fallen for it. She couldn't believe that he could behave this way towards her but, there again, he had a lot to gain, didn't he?

The thought that he was prepared to put Dee's happiness above hers and Izzy's was too painful. She had to make a conscious effort not to show how devastated she felt. 'We've just admitted ten-year-old twins who have both suffered severe asthma attacks. Their sats are down and A and E wants them monitored overnight. The family is here on holiday so we don't have full case histories for them yet.'

'I take it they're on a treatment regime?' he said, instantly focusing on the problem.

'Yes. And their mother seems to be very capable, too,' she replied, resenting the fact that he could instantly switch his mind back on track. Did he behave like this with Dee? she wondered. Or did he find it far more difficult to remain focused when he was with the woman he really loved?

Her breath caught on a sob and she cleared her throat when she saw him look at her. 'A and E have asked the GP to fax their notes through but I imagine their mother can fill in a lot of the background details.'

'I'd better have a word with her first, then.' He got up and went to the door, pausing when she went to follow him out. 'Are you all right, Lucy?' he said softly, searching her face with eyes that appeared to be filled with tender concern.

'Fine,' she said shortly. She wasn't going to allow herself to be duped again like she'd been duped last night.

Her heart caught as the memory of what had happened came rushing back while she made her way from the office. She had honestly thought that he had loved her last night and that the way he had behaved with her then—so tender, so caring, so passionate—had been proof of that. Now she could see that it had been all an act, a means to get what he wanted, and what he wanted most was Dee's happiness.

She didn't think she would ever forgive him for what he'd done. He had taken her heart and trampled all over it, not once but twice. All she could do now was to make sure that he didn't get the chance to do the same to Izzy. He might want Izzy now for Dee's sake but what would happen if Dee discovered that she couldn't love the little girl? Would Izzy then become surplus to their requirements?

The thought of her precious child suffering the kind of heartache she had to endure was more than Lucy could bear. No matter what Connor said or what claims he made from now on, she wasn't going to believe him!

Connor could tell that there was something wrong with Lucy but he wasn't sure what had happened to upset her. He knew that the hospital's gossip mill had been working overtime and that everyone must know that he was Izzy's father, so was it that which was worrying her? Although it didn't bother him, he could understand it if Lucy found it distressing to know that people were talking about them.

She was a very private person and he wished he could have spared her all this embarrassment. Maybe they should do something to squash all the rumours? If they got married then that would soon put an end to the speculation, but how would she feel about the idea of marrying him?

Connor frowned as he followed her to the relatives' room. He had no idea how she felt about marriage because they had never discussed it. Marriage had never been on his agenda in the past but it was on it now—and at the top of the list, too. He smiled in amazement when he realised how much he had changed. He'd switched from being a career-orientated bachelor to a prospective husband almost overnight! Now all he had to do was to convince Lucy that he was serious and he could make his new dreams come true.

It was a tantalising thought and he found it difficult to put it out of his mind as he introduced himself to Mrs Gentry. He could see how upset the poor woman was and smiled encouragingly at her. 'Your boys are in the best possible place so try not to worry. I know how frightening asthma attacks can be and it's doubly bad for you, but the twins will be fine.'

'I've never seen them this bad before, Dr Mackenzie.' The woman wiped her eyes. 'I can't understand it because I'm always so careful. I check their peak flow reading three times a day and make sure they take their medication exactly on time. Their routine hasn't changed just because we're on holiday.'

'It isn't your fault that this has happened,' he assured her. 'Can you give me some idea of their treatment regime and the drugs they're currently taking?'

'I brought their medication with me.'

Mrs Gentry opened her bag and showed him the drugs. Connor nodded. Both boys were taking corticosteroids, which were highly effective in controlling the symptoms of asthma when used on a daily basis. Although corticosteroids could cause side effects, it was less likely when they were inhaled because only very small amounts were absorbed into the bloodstream.

'That's fine,' he said, handing the medication back to her. 'I am certainly not going to interfere with the treatment your own doctor has prescribed for them. What I would like to do, though, is to find out what might have triggered the attacks today.'

'I wish I knew!' Mrs Gentry exclaimed. 'We're staying in our own caravan so I know that it's been thoroughly cleaned. I use anti-allergen covers on all the soft furnishings as well as the bedding, and we have blinds instead of curtains because they hold less dust. I also disinfect the floors as well as the worktops at least twice a day. My husband says that you could eat your dinner off our caravan floor because it's so clean!'

'And do you do the same at home?' he asked.

'Oh, yes! I always have ever since the boys were born. You'd never find a germ in my house.'

'It certainly sounds as though you are very thorough, Mrs Gentry.' He smiled at her, although he increasingly suspected that the root of the twins' problems could lie in their mother's fastidiousness. Over-zealous cleaning could lead to a lack of tolerance for everyday allergens, which in turn could trigger an asthma attack. He decided that he would have a word with her GP about it and stood up.

'I'm going to take a look at the boys so I'll come back and see you later. Get yourself a cup of tea and try to relax—everything is going to be fine.'

He nodded to Lucy to indicate that he would like her to accompany him and they left the relatives' room. She didn't say a word as they walked along the corridor and it wasn't a comfortable silence either. Connor could tell from her tight-lipped expression that there was something bothering her so he stopped when they came to the office.

'It's obvious something's worrying you. Why don't we go in here and talk about it?'

'I don't think so.'

She carried on walking and ignored him as she made her way to the ward. Connor followed her inside but he had to admit that he was confused. Maybe she was upset at the thought of all the gossip that was circulating, but was it only that? Or was there something else troubling her?

She'd seemed to accept the fact that he'd had to leave her last night to come to work so surely it couldn't be that which had upset her, yet what other explanation could there be? As he approached the twins' beds he realised that he needed to sort this out as quickly as possible. The last thing he wanted was for there to be any more misunderstandings between them.

Lucy was relieved when Connor left to attend the finance meeting. It had been unbearable to be near him after what had happened. Fortunately, she was kept busy after that so the afternoon flew past and then it was time to leave.

She collected Izzy from the crèche and drove straight home. She had been planning to stop off on the way to do some shopping but she was too tired and too upset to bother. She made them scrambled eggs for their tea, although most of hers ended up in the bin because she didn't feel like eating.

Izzy chattered away in baby talk while she washed the dishes. The little girl was unaware of what was happening and that was the way Lucy intended the situation to remain. Izzy wasn't going to be used as a pawn by her father—she wouldn't allow it, even though she knew that she would have a fight on her hands if she tried to stop Connor seeing their daughter. However, no matter what he threatened to do, she wasn't going to budge. He wasn't going to have anything more to do with Izzy if she had her way!

When the doorbell rang at ten minutes past eight that evening, Lucy knew that she had been expecting it. Connor must be eager to finalise things now that he thought he had paved the way towards getting what he wanted. She got up and went to open the door. The sooner they sorted this out the better for her, too.

'Hi!'

He smiled at her as he stepped into the hall and she felt her heart shrivel up when she saw the warmth in his eyes. He was a superb actor—she had to give him that. If she hadn't known what he was planning then she would have believed he really cared about her. But she was just another pawn in this game he was playing. He didn't really give a damn about her.

Lucy didn't say a word as she turned and walked into the sitting-room. Her feelings didn't matter now. She needed to reserve all her energy for what really mattered, which was Izzy and the need to protect her.

'What's wrong, Lucy?' He followed her into the room, catching hold of her arm when she didn't reply so that she was forced to stop. 'Lucy, please!'

'I don't want you to see Izzy again,' she said flatly, not even bothering to answer his question. He didn't care about her: he cared about Dee. The thought brought tears to her eyes but she blinked them away. She wouldn't cry in front of him, wouldn't ever make herself that vulnerable again.

'What do you mean?' He spun her round to face him. 'What's going on? Why have you suddenly decided that I can't see Izzy?'

'Because I will not allow you to use her, Connor,' she spat back, pulling herself free.

'*Use* her? Look, I don't know what's happened—'

'I overheard you and Dee talking today.' All of a sudden she couldn't take any more. She didn't want him to lie to her again. He had done enough of that last night. He may not have said that he'd loved her but she'd thought he had meant that by the way he had made love to her. And she couldn't begin to explain how wretched she felt about allowing herself to be deceived that way.

'I see. So what exactly did you hear?'

His tone was harsh, his face set into such stern lines that a shiver ran through her. She could tell how angry he was but if anyone had the right to feel angry then it was her and not him!

'I heard you telling her that it didn't matter if the child wasn't hers, that she would still love it because she loved its father.'

'And you thought I was talking about Izzy? You think I want Izzy in my life so I can give Dee a child?'

'Yes! What other child could you have been talking about? And everyone knows that you and Dee are having a relationship. It's been the talk of the hospital!' she said bitterly.

'And you believe it, too, do you? Even after last night you still think that Dee and I are having an affair?' He laughed softly but there was no trace of humour in the sound. 'It's amazing, isn't it? You'd rather believe a lot of foolish gossip than what I've told you. And I thought you had faith in me.'

'Are you saying that it isn't true? That I imagined that whole conversation?' she demanded, because he was making it sound as though she was the one at fault.

'Not at all. If you heard it then it must be true, mustn't it?'

He swung round but Lucy couldn't let him leave like this. She needed to hear it from his own lips what he had done. 'So you're admitting that the only reason you came back here was for Izzy?'

'That's right.' He glanced back and she recoiled when she saw the contempt in his eyes. 'I came back for Izzy. So if you think that I am going to give her up, then you are mistaken. I am her father and that is one fact that you cannot change to suit yourself, Lucy. And because I am her father, I will do whatever it takes to gain access to her.'

CHAPTER FOURTEEN

CONNOR could scarcely believe what was happening. How could a few short hours have made such a huge difference? he wondered as he let himself out of the flat. Last night he'd been so sure that Lucy had trusted him but obviously he'd been wrong.

She couldn't trust him if she believed that he had planned to use their daughter! She couldn't trust him if she believed that he was having an affair with another woman! And if she didn't trust him then she couldn't love him either.

His vision blurred as he got into his car and he wasn't ashamed to admit that he felt like crying. All those dreams he'd had for their future together would amount to nothing now. There wouldn't be a home and a family, a happy-ever-after for him and Lucy. There would be just bitterness and suspicion, and he didn't know how he was going to stand it. It made him wonder if he should accept her decision not to let him have any more contact with Izzy. Heaven knew, he didn't want to hurt her any more, yet the thought of giving up his rights to his child was more than he could bear. He needed to be there for Izzy, no matter how much Lucy might hate having him around.

The thought of what was going to happen in the coming weeks plagued him so that he found it impossible to sleep. He was bone tired when he went into work the following day and it didn't help that the first person he saw was Lucy. She bade him a curt good morning then went into the office and closed the door, making it clear that she didn't intend to talk to him.

Connor's mouth thinned as he followed her into the room. It was going to be hell on earth if she behaved like this. Maybe she did believe that she had a genuine grievance but he'd be damned if he would allow her to treat him like a leper while they were in work!

'We need to lay down some ground rules,' he said grimly as he strode over to the desk. 'I am the head of this department and I expect you to behave in a suitably professional manner towards me when we are at work. Is that clear?'

'Perfectly, sir. Is there anything else you wish to say?'

She stared back at him and it was all he could do not to apologise when he saw the pain in her eyes. He knew that if he explained the background to that conversation between him and Dee, it would make her see that she'd been wrong about him, but he also knew how pointless it would be. Even if she believed him, it wouldn't really change anything. Lucy had to know in her own mind that she could trust him or the same thing would happen again in the future. He couldn't bear to live under a cloud of suspicion, always wondering if today would be the day when she lost her faith in him for good. Maybe it was his fault that she felt this way, but he couldn't rewrite the past. He just had to live with the consequences. And it might be too much to hope that a relationship that didn't have trust as its foundation could survive.

'Yes, that's all.' He strode to the door then glanced back,

deliberately erasing any trace of emotion from his face. 'I'd like to make an early start on the ward round today. Can you check that Nicholas and Simon Gentry's notes have arrived? If they haven't, can you chase up their GP for me, please.'

'Of course, sir.'

Her tone was bland yet he heard the pain it held and his hand clenched on the handle before he forced himself to open the door. 'Thank you.'

He left the office and made his way upstairs to find his team. They were in the residents' lounge, enjoying a last cup of coffee, so he told them curtly to be in his office in five minutes' time and left. As he opened the door to his own sanctum, Connor felt a wave of weariness wash over him. If this was an indication of what was to come then he wasn't looking forward to it one little bit. Even though he had come back to England fully expecting to have to fight for his rights regarding Izzy, it wasn't a prospect he had ever relished. Now it appealed even less because now he understood how he really felt about Izzy's mother. He loved Lucy and wished with all his heart that he had never let her go, but she didn't feel the same about him and never would. And every minute of every day that he had to spend with her was going to be sheer torture.

Connor was terse to the point of rudeness during the ward round. Lucy could tell from everyone's expressions that they were wondering what was going on. He was little short of scathing when Tom got some basic facts wrong and not much kinder to Amanda when she stumbled her way through a potted history of the twins' asthma. It wasn't what he actually said but the way he said it, so coldly, so distantly, so…so lacking in emotion. She knew why he was behaving that way, of course, and she felt racked with guilt as well as anguish. It wasn't fair that everyone had to suffer because of her!

'Am I glad that's over!' Amanda exclaimed as soon as Connor had disappeared. 'He must have been lulling us into a false sense of security for the past couple of weeks. I believe everything anyone has ever told me about him now!'

'You have to admit that he's really clued up,' Martin put in, obviously trying to pour oil onto very troubled waters. 'He'd already highlighted the fact that Mrs Gentry was probably making matters worse for her boys by doing all that cleaning before we'd seen the GP's notes and those comments he'd made when he'd last seen the twins. I mean, Connor had only spent a few minutes with the woman and he'd still picked up on it,' he added when Amanda looked less than impressed.

'He might be the best paediatrician in the whole wide world but he's definitely lacking in the social skills department. Pity help any poor woman who gets involved with him is all I can say— Oops, sorry, Lucy. That wasn't very tactful of me.' Amanda blushed. She had obviously heard the rumours about Izzy being Connor's daughter.

Lucy shrugged. She didn't want to make the other woman feel uncomfortable. 'You're entitled to your opinions, Amanda. There's no need to apologise.'

'Hmm, maybe not but thanks all the same.'

Amanda beat a hasty retreat, and Lucy sighed. It was going to be very difficult if people thought that they had to walk on eggshells around her. So she'd had a relationship with Connor and had ended up having his child—she wouldn't let it dictate what happened for the rest of her life!

It was a wonderful sentiment but very difficult to put into

practice. In the days following, she soon realised that her relationship with Connor had had an effect on how people thought of her. She tried to carry on as normal but the constant looks and comments started to wear her down. She began to think seriously about finding another job, although she had no intention of running away. She had firmly scotched that idea and would tell Connor where she was going if she did decide to leave. It would be up to him then if he continued fighting for access to Izzy.

He had said nothing more on the subject, although she wasn't foolish enough to think that he had given up. He was probably waiting until Dee made up her mind about how she felt before putting his plans into action, and that was another depressing thought. Her life and Izzy's might all hinge on the whims of another woman so she was glad that Dee wasn't needed at work. The less she saw of Dee as well as Connor, the better!

After a short dry spell, the rain started again and this time it caused mayhem. Overnight some parts of the town were flooded and Lucy ended up with a wall of sandbags piled outside her front door to keep out the water. The car park closest to the old section of the hospital was flooded when she arrived at work so she had to park elsewhere and carry Izzy to the crèche. Then, when she got to the ward, she discovered that Sandra had phoned to say that she couldn't get in because the buses had stopped running. It meant that she and Alison would have to cope on their own that morning, no easy task when the ward was full.

Lucy set to work on the morning obs and had got halfway round when there was a tremendous crash from outside. She ran to the window to see what had happened and gasped when she saw clouds of dust billowing from the old part of the building where the crèche was housed.

'What's happened?' Alison demanded, peering over her shoulder. 'Oh, no! Part of the old building has collapsed!'

Lucy thrust the files she was holding into Alison's hands. 'I have to go and see if Izzy's all right. She's in the crèche…'

Her voice dried up as she ran towards the door. She could hear the office phone ringing but she ignored it as she raced along the corridor. She had to get to Izzy and make sure that she was safe!

A lot of people must have had the same idea because there was a crowd running towards the old section of the building by the time Lucy got down to the car park. She followed them as fast as she could, her fear intensifying as she got closer and saw what had happened. The end wall had fallen away, leaving the rest of the building in a very precarious position. There were people rushing about all over the place and she could hear sirens in the distance, but all she could think about was getting to Izzy.

'Lucy!'

She swung round when she heard Connor shouting her name. She could see the terror in his eyes as he ran towards her. 'Where's Izzy? Is she in there?' he demanded, skidding to a stop.

'Yes! I've got to get to her!' She tried to push past him so she could get into the building but he wouldn't let her pass.

'I'll get her. You must stay here. Understand? You have got to stay here.'

'But Izzy needs me—'

'I will get her for you, Lucy. I swear I will. Just trust me—please.'

He squeezed her hands then turned and ran into the ruins

of the building. Lucy put her hand over her mouth as terror gripped her. Connor would do his best but would he get to Izzy in time, would he be able to save their precious child?

A sob broke from her lips at the thought of losing Izzy but she forced herself not to give in to the panic that gripped her. There were other parents arriving now but the security staff had set up a cordon and they stopped anyone else from going inside the building. The fire brigade arrived and a team was sent inside. The minutes ticked past with agonising slowness then a great cheer erupted when the crew appeared with a number of children and some members of the crèche's staff. Lucy hurried forward, pushing her way through the crowd to find her daughter, but there was no sign of Izzy or Connor.

She ran over to one of the nursery nurses, hoping she might be able to tell her what was happening. 'What about the babies? They're in a separate room so are they all right?'

'I don't know.' The girl looked upset. 'I was in the hall, helping some of the toddlers off the slide. I just grabbed as many of them as I could and ran. I'm sorry but I don't know what's happened to the rest.'

Another mother came over to speak to the girl so Lucy moved aside. More children were being brought out now and her heart leapt in relief when she saw that one of the firemen was carrying two of the babies. She ran over to him but neither of them was Izzy.

'My baby's in there,' she told him frantically. 'Her father's gone inside to find her—did you see him?'

'No, but there's a lot of dust in there so it's difficult to see what's happening.' He glanced round. 'Ask one of the other guys—they might have seen him.'

Lucy hurried over to another group of firefighters but

they hadn't seen Connor either. One of the staff was marking off the names of all the children on a register and there seemed to be just three missing now—all of them young babies who had been in the most severely damaged section of the crèche.

Lucy could see the sympathy on the other parents' faces as they collected their children and hurried them away, but she wasn't going to give up hope yet. Connor would get Izzy out—he would! He loved her too much to let anything happen to her!

The thought came out of nowhere, yet she knew it was true. Connor loved Izzy for herself and not because of what she might mean for him and Dee. That was why he had risked his own life to save her. He loved their precious child every bit as much as she did and she'd been wrong to say that he couldn't have anything more to do with her.

Lucy wrapped her arms around herself as her fear grew. She had to hold onto the belief that Connor would bring their daughter safely back to her. It was all she had and she wanted it to be true, but she also wanted Connor to be safe, too. She loved him, as well—so much. Even though he could never love her, she couldn't bear to imagine any harm coming to him. A world without Connor in it would be such a lonely place.

There was a sudden flurry of activity around the entrance to the building and she swung round when she heard someone shouting for a stretcher. A couple of paramedics raced inside and Lucy held her breath as she waited to see what was happening.

Some members of the fire crew suddenly emerged from the ruins carrying the last of the children, and she cried out in relief when she saw that one of them was Izzy. She ran forward and took her in her arms, covering her face with kisses. The little girl was covered in dust and bits of plaster but she didn't appear to have been injured; she even started laughing when Lucy kissed her.

'Let's get him into A and E, stat!'

Lucy swung round when she heard one of the A and E staff shouting instructions and felt her heart turn over when she realised he was talking about Connor. The paramedics were carrying him out of the building on a stretcher and they wasted no time as they hurried towards the accident and emergency department. She had to run to catch up with them.

'What's happened to him?' she demanded, her breath catching when she saw how pale and still he looked.

'Crush injuries,' the registrar told her succinctly. 'It looked as though he was trying to protect the kids by holding up a section of the wall. We just managed to get them out before it caved in, but he wasn't so lucky.'

He didn't say anything else as he led the paramedic crew into the A and E department, but he didn't need to. Lucy could picture the scene for herself and her eyes filled with tears at the thought of what Connor had done. He had risked his own life for Izzy and the other babies, and it was a measure of the man he was—strong, honest, true. All she could hope now was that she would be able to tell him how grateful she was. And after she'd told him that then she would also make it clear that she would never stop him seeing Izzy. He had saved their daughter's life and he had earned that right.

She took a deep breath. Even though she knew it was what she wanted to do, it still hurt. But if Connor wanted to help Dee by allowing her to share in his daughter's future, she wouldn't stand in his way.

* * *

Someone was playing the drums inside his skull.

Connor groaned as he opened his eyes. He couldn't remember having a headache like this since he had been a student and had gone out to celebrate passing his finals. And even then his head hadn't ached *this* badly.

'Connor? Can you hear me?'

He frowned when he heard Lucy talking to him. She sounded so distressed that he could only assume that she felt as bad as he did. Had they been out celebrating and drunk rather too much wine? But celebrating what?

He slowly turned his head and moaned when the thumping inside his head just got worse. 'I swear I'm never going to touch another drop of alcohol,' he muttered, closing his eyes in the vain hope that it might make him feel better.

'Oh, Connor, darling, it isn't a hangover that's making you feel like that! Don't you remember what happened?'

Connor wasn't sure what to deal with first. The fact that Lucy had called him 'darling' definitely required a response of some sort, but her question also seemed to deserve some attention. Exactly what was he supposed to remember?

He forced the pain to recede while he tried to work it out and gasped as he suddenly remembered what had happened. Opening his eyes, he stared at Lucy in horror. 'Izzy...!'

'She's fine, Connor. There wasn't a scratch on her or on the other two babies.' Tears rolled down her face as she bent over and kissed him on the cheek. 'Thank you so much for what you did. I don't know what I would have done if you hadn't found her...'

A sob suddenly caught up with her and he felt his own eyes fill with tears too as all the fear caught up with him. 'I was so scared, Lucy,' he whispered. 'I thought I was going to lose her…'

He couldn't go on but he didn't need to explain. Lucy understood how he felt because she had gone through the same agony with him. His heart ached when it struck him that it was a bond they would always share. No matter what happened between them, they would always worry about Izzy, always want what was best for her. They both loved their precious daughter so much and it seemed wrong that they should let a stupid misunderstanding get in the way of them working together to secure her future.

Lifting his hand, he touched Lucy's cheek. 'I love Izzy and I will never do anything to hurt her. I know you find it difficult to trust me, Lucy, but it's true.'

'I believe you.' She drew back and smiled at him, and Connor felt his heart give an almighty jerk when he saw the warmth in her eyes. He had never thought he would see her look at him that way again and the relief made him feel so weak that he couldn't speak.

'I really do believe you,' she said urgently, mistaking his silence for disbelief. She gripped his hand and held it tightly and he could tell that she was on the verge of breaking down. 'I know that you will never do anything to harm Izzy so if…if you feel that it would help you and Dee to spend time with her, I swear I won't stand in your way.'

'Thank you,' he said softly, overwhelmed by emotion. 'You have no idea how much it means to me to hear you say that.'

'I think I can guess,' she murmured, avoiding his eyes.

'I'm sure you can. But you would be wrong.' He smiled when he saw the confusion on her face as she looked at him. 'Dee and I are not having an affair and we never have been having one. Dee is engaged to a really great guy called Mike Wilson, who happens to be a friend of mine from Boston.'

'A friend? But I don't understand! If you and Dee aren't involved then why were you trying to persuade her that she would grow to love Izzy?'

'I wasn't.' He sighed softly. 'Think about what you heard, Lucy. Did I ever mention Izzy's name?'

'No…' she said slowly.

'No,' he said firmly. 'I can't go into too much detail because it's not up to me to discuss Dee's situation. Suffice to say that Mike had come up with a solution to the problem of them not being able to have a family and had flown over to England to talk to her about it.' He shrugged. 'I told her what I thought of the idea—that was all.'

'So the baby you mentioned wasn't Izzy?'

'No. Izzy is our child—yours and mine. And I was never, ever trying to make use of her in any way. All I want to do is to make sure she is safe and happy and that I can play a part in her future, even if it's only a very small one.'

'I got it completely wrong, didn't I?' she said brokenly. 'You were telling me the truth all along and I didn't believe you.'

'I don't blame you, Lucy. If anyone's to blame then it's me.' He cleared his throat but it was hard to conquer the feeling of despair that was creeping up on him. 'The biggest mistake I ever made was leaving you. I should have listened to my heart instead of my head and stayed here.'

'What do you mean?'

'That I love you. That's why I went away, in fact. I knew that I was falling in love with you and I was terrified.' He closed his eyes because he couldn't bear to look at her in case she didn't believe him.

'I love you, too, Connor. I always have.'

The words were softly spoken yet they had the impact of a speeding bullet and his eyes flew open again. 'You love me?'

'Yes.' She smiled at him. 'That's why I've been so desperate to keep you at arm's length. I was afraid of getting hurt again, you see.'

'I will never hurt you!' he promised, and there was a world of conviction in his voice. He gripped her hand. 'I know how hard it must be for you to believe me—'

'It isn't.' She bent and kissed him gently on the mouth and there were tears of joy in her eyes this time when she looked at him. 'Now that you've told me that you love me, it's the easiest thing in the world to believe in you.'

He lifted her hand to his mouth and kissed it. 'I don't deserve you, my love. I just wish I'd told you how I really felt the other night. I wanted to so desperately but I was afraid.'

'Afraid I wouldn't believe you?'

'Partly. I was more afraid that the words wouldn't be enough. People told me things when I was a child and they didn't mean them…'

He couldn't go on but Lucy didn't need him to explain. He could tell from her expression that she had filled in the gaps. When she leant over and kissed him this time, Connor felt a great surge of relief wash away any fears he might have had. Lucy understood because she cared about him. She loved him and she believed in him. He would never need to prove his worth to her because she already believed he was worth her love.

He couldn't begin to explain how wonderful it made him feel to know that, and didn't try. Why waste time on words when actions could speak for him? He returned the kiss, letting his lips meld with hers so that they were both breathless when they drew apart. Lucy ran a trembling hand over her hair and blushed.

'It's a good job they put you in a private room or we'd have an audience right now!'

'Let them look,' he said smugly, enjoying feeling loved and wanted for the first time in his entire life. 'We might be able to show them a thing or two!'

'Cheeky!' She laughed at that then suddenly sobered. 'Joking apart, though, you must take things easy until you're better.'

'What was the verdict?' he asked, realising for the first time that he hadn't given much thought to the injuries he'd suffered. He wriggled his fingers and toes and breathed a sigh of relief when everything worked as it should. Apart from a lot of aches and pains, he didn't feel *that* bad.

'They were worried in case you were suffering from crush syndrome at first—apparently one of the internal walls, which you'd been holding up over the babies to protect them, collapsed on you.'

She shuddered and he gently squeezed her hand. 'They're OK, though, aren't they? The babies, I mean?'

'They're fine…every single one of them.' She managed to smile at him but he could tell the effort it cost her. 'Anyway, A and E ran all the usual tests to see if there were protein pigments in your bloodstream from any damaged muscles and there weren't. Your kidney function wasn't impaired either so the consensus is that you've been extremely lucky. Apart from a mild concussion, you seem to have escaped relatively unscathed, but you still need to take life easy for a few days.'

'Mild? *Mild!*' He hammed it up for all he was worth, wanting to take her mind off what had happened. He knew how he would have felt if the situation had been reversed and couldn't bear to imagine her suffering. 'I'll have you know this is the worst headache I have ever had in my entire life. In fact, if I had to rate it on a scale of one to ten, it would be a definite eleven!'

'In that case, you need to rest.' She dropped a kiss on his lips and stood up. Connor stared at her in shock.

'You aren't leaving me?'

'I'm afraid so. I was only supposed to stay for ten minutes and it's way past that. Any minute now, I'll be thrown out.'

Connor groaned when the door opened and a nurse appeared. 'You two are working hand in glove,' he accused them.

Lucy grinned when the other nurse looked questioningly at her. 'Temper tantrum. Take no notice. I'm used to dealing with this kind of thing on Paeds.'

The other nurse chuckled. She told Lucy her time was up then closed the door. Connor looked imploringly at her but she hardened her heart.

'There's no point looking at me like that. You need to rest and I intend to see that you do so.' She walked to the door then turned and blew him a kiss. 'That will have to keep you going until I come back.'

Connor was still grumbling when she closed the door and she smiled as she left the assessment ward. He could grumble all he liked but she wasn't going to give in. She wanted him fit and well so they could get on with the rest of their lives together. Him, her and Izzy…their daughter!

Three months later…

'Lucy, are you ready? The car's here.'

Connor hurried to the door then stopped when it opened and Lucy appeared. For a second he couldn't seem to catch his breath as he stared at her. She looked so beautiful in the soft cream dress she had chosen to wear for their wedding. He was useless at describing women's clothes but it certainly pressed all the right buttons so far as he was concerned!

He stepped forward and took her in his arms. 'You look stunning,' he said, his voice grating with emotion. He nuzzled her cheek because he didn't want to spoil her lipstick by kissing her, but she turned and kissed him instead.

'So I pass muster, do I?' she said, smiling up at him.

'Oh, yes. You most certainly do.' He kissed her hungrily, wondering if any man had ever felt as he did at that moment. In half an hour's time he and Lucy would exchange their vows and promise to stay with each other until they died.

Once such a promise would have been unthinkable but now he knew it was going to happen and that it was going to last. Lucy was going to stay with him and he would stay with her and nothing—absolutely nothing!—would separate them again. He only hoped that he would live to be a hundred because it would mean that he had all those years to spend loving her. Yet in his heart he knew that not even a lifetime with Lucy would be enough.

He kissed her again then stepped back when he heard the sound of a car horn. 'Sounds like our driver is getting impatient. Shall I fetch Izzy?'

'Please. She's all ready.'

Lucy smiled as he hurried out of the room. Their wedding was to be a very simple affair because that was what she'd wanted. Her family would be there and a few friends, including Dee and her fiancé, who had flown over from Boston specially to attend. The service was being held in the local church and there would be a small reception afterwards but that was it. Neither she nor Connor had wanted a lot of fuss.

'Here she is. And she's as gorgeous as her mummy.'

She turned when Connor came back with Izzy. He held out his hand, and she could see the love in his eyes. 'Ready to go now?'

'More than ready.' Lucy took his hand then kissed him on the cheek. 'I love you,' she whispered.

'And I love you too, my darling.' He kissed her back then kissed Izzy as well. 'Let's go and make this official, then we can get on with our lives as a proper family. I don't know about you two girls, but I can't wait!'

0706/03a

MILLS & BOON

Live the emotion

_Medical
romance™

THE SICILIAN DOCTOR'S PROPOSAL
by Sarah Morgan

Mediterranean Doctors
Passionate about life, love and medicine.

Dr Alice Anderson doesn't believe in love – no
matter how much the new doctor Dr Giovanni
Moretti tries to persuade her otherwise. Gio's
feelings for Alice are undeniably strong. But will
the impossibly charming Sicilian be able to make
Alice realise that she has done the unthinkable
– fallen in love?

THE FIREFIGHTER'S FIANCÉ by Kate Hardy

Kelsey Watson loves her firefighting job, is happily
single and she has a wonderful friend and house-
mate in paramedic Matt Fraser. Then Matt notices
how deeply a fierce fire in a local school affects
Kelsey. And as he tries to help her, a deeper
connection between them emerges…

EMERGENCY BABY by Alison Roberts

As part of the Specialist Emergency Response Team,
paramedic Samantha Moore has always been one
of the boys. But now her biological clock is ticking
– and she wants a baby! Sam begins to search for the
perfect father…and discovers him right under her
nose: her SERT partner, Alex! Soon Sam begins to
see Alex as the perfect husband too.

On sale 4th August 2006

*Available at WHSmith, Tesco, ASDA, Borders, Eason,
Sainsbury's and most bookshops*

www.millsandboon.co.uk

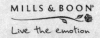

MILLS & BOON®

Live the emotion

Medical
romance™

0706/03b

BRIDE AT BAY HOSPITAL by *Meredith Webber*

Bad boy Sam Agostini left the bay thirteen years
ago, leaving Nurse Megan Anstey broken-hearted.
Now he is back, still devastatingly handsome, still
undeniably charming, and a highly respected doctor.
As Sam fights to make up to Megan for his past, new
secrets start to bubble to the surface…

THE FLIGHT DOCTOR'S ENGAGEMENT
by *Laura Iding*

Air Rescue:
High flying doctors – High altitude medical drama

Flight doctor Zach Taylor is intrigued by his partner
– fiery paramedic Jenna Reed. There is more to
Jenna than meets the eye – and he is intrigued by her
determination to rescue everyone and everything.
Zach can see that it's Jenna herself who needs saving
– his plan is to do exactly that and, hopefully, also
win her heart!

IN HIS SPECIAL CARE by *Lucy Clark*

Despite being Mt Black Hospital's only full-time GP,
Dr Claire Neilson always finds time for her patients.
But Claire doesn't let anyone care for her…until
the new specialist – incredibly handsome, enigmatic
Dr Declan Silvermark arrives in the small Australian
town and turns her carefully ordered world upside
down…

On sale 4th August 2006

*Available at WHSmith, Tesco, ASDA, Borders, Eason,
Sainsbury's and most bookshops*

www.millsandboon.co.uk

0906_TEN_R.ELAUNCH

THE SERIES YOU LOVE IS GETTING EVEN BETTER

This September, Tender Romance™ is getting a new look and improving on the stories you know and love.

Tender Romance is becoming *Mills & Boon® Romance.* You'll find your favourite authors and more of the stories you love— we're just making them better!

Watch for the new, improved Mills & Boon Romance series at your favourite bookseller this autumn.

MILLS & BOON®

Romance

Pure romance, pure emotion

0706/155

**Extra medical drama for
your money!**

Maggie Kingsley and Laura Iding

3 stories set in the exciting world of A&E

***Where passions run high and love
and lives are on the line!***

Emergency:
Love

On sale from 4th August 2006

*Available at most branches of WHSmith, Tesco, ASDA,
Borders, Eason, Sainsbury's and most bookshops*

Visit www.millsandboon.co.uk

0706/05a

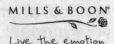

MILLS & BOON®

Live the emotion

In August 2006 Mills & Boon bring
back two of their classic collections, each
featuring three favourite romances by our
bestselling authors…

The Counts of Calvani

by
Lucy Gordon

Featuring
The Venetian Playboy's Bride
The Italian Millionaire's Marriage
The Tuscan Tycoon's Wife

**Make sure you buy these
irresistible stories!**

On sale 4th August 2006

*Available at WHSmith, Tesco, ASDA, Borders, Eason,
Sainsbury's and most bookshops*
www.millsandboon.co.uk

MILLS & BOON®

Live the emotion

0706/05b

Their Secret Child

Featuring
The Latin Lover's Secret Child by Jane Porter
Her Baby Secret by Kim Lawrence
The Greek Tycoon's Secret Child
by Cathy Williams
Make sure you buy these irresistible stories!

On sale 4th August 2006

*Available at WHSmith, Tesco, ASDA, Borders, Eason,
Sainsbury's and most bookshops*
www.millsandboon.co.uk

4 FREE

BOOKS AND A SURPRISE GIFT!

We would like to take this opportunity to thank you for reading this Mills & Boon® book by offering you the chance to take FOUR more specially selected titles from the Medical Romance™ series absolutely FREE! We're also making this offer to introduce you to the benefits of the Reader Service™—

- ★ FREE home delivery
- ★ FREE gifts and competitions
- ★ FREE monthly Newsletter
- ★ Exclusive Reader Service offers
- ★ Books available before they're in the shops

Accepting these FREE books and gift places you under no obligation to buy, you may cancel at any time, even after receiving your free shipment. Simply complete your details below and return the entire page to the address below. You don't even need a stamp!

YES! Please send me 4 free Medical Romance books and a surprise gift. I understand that unless you hear from me, I will receive 6 superb new titles every month for just £2.80 each, postage and packing free. I am under no obligation to purchase any books and may cancel my subscription at any time. The free books and gift will be mine to keep in any case.

M6ZED

Ms/Mrs/Miss/Mr .... Initials ....

BLOCK CAPITALS PLEASE

Surname ....

Address ....

....

.... Postcode ....

Send this whole page to:
UK: FREEPOST CN81, Croydon, CR9 3WZ

Offer valid in UK only and is not available to current Reader service subscribers to this series. Overseas and Eire please write for details. We reserve the right to refuse an application and applicants must be aged 18 years or over. Only one application per household. Terms and prices subject to change without notice. Offer expires 31st October 2006. As a result of this application, you may receive offers from Harlequin Mills & Boon and other carefully selected companies. If you would prefer not to share in this opportunity please write to The Data Manager, PO Box 676, Richmond, TW9 1WU.

Mills & Boon® is a registered trademark owned by Harlequin Mills & Boon Limited.
Medical Romance™ is being used as a trademark. The Reader Service™ is being used as a trademark.